desert passage

desert passage

a novel
by
P.S. Carrillo

PIÑATA BOOKS
ARTE PÚBLICO PRESS
HOUSTON, TEXAS

Desert Passage is funded in part by grants from the City of Houston through the Houston Arts Alliance and by the Exemplar Program, a program of Americans for the Arts in collaboration with the LarsonAllen Public Services Group, funded by the Ford Foundation.

Piñata Books are full of surprises!

Piñata Books

An imprint of
Arte Público Press
University of Houston
452 Cullen Performance Hall
Houston, Texas 77204-2004

Cover art by Giovanni Mora
Cover design by Mora Des!gn

Carrillo, P. S.
    Desert Passage / by P. S. Carrillo.
       p.   cm.
    Summary: Two cousins go on an impromptu journey from northern Arizona to Santa Fe, New Mexico when their grandmother gets sick, and their experiences along the way give them invaluable insights about life, family, and themselves.
    ISBN: 978-1-55885-517-5 (alk. paper)
    [1. Coming of age—Fiction. 2. Voyages and travels—Fiction. 3. Cousins—Fiction. 4. Deserts—Fiction. 5. Southwest, New—Fiction.] I. Title.
    PZ7.C23457De 2008
    [Fic]—dc22

                                   2008017161
                                      CPI

8 9 0 1 2 3 4 5 6 7   10 9 8 7 6 5 4 3 2 1

For every young man
who has dared to dream
of a road leading to somewhere.

chapter 1

Miguel and Ramón stood staring at the stacks of boxes and luggage that covered the concrete driveway.

"Dad said to load the boxes first, then the luggage," reminded Miguel, picking up one of the lighter boxes.

"Yeah, but do the boxes all go to one side, then the luggage?" asked Ramón.

"How am I supposed to know?" Miguel answered his cousin. "Let's just put the stuff in, it's getting hot out here, man."

One by one they lifted the heavy boxes and loaded the over-packed luggage into the back of the truck. The garage door was open and they could see Rodrigo going in and out of the house bringing out more boxes to pack.

"How much more is there?" Miguel complained.

"I'll go get it," sighed Ramón. He walked slowly over to the newly stacked boxes and picked one up. In the corner of the garage a pile of stuff caught his eye. A large assortment of camping and fishing equipment was gathering spiderwebs and dust.

"Hey, remember when we used to go on trips with Grandpa?" Ramón said, walking back to the truck.

"Yeah," Miguel replied mournfully, "I wish we were going on a trip now."

After the back of the SUV was packed, Rodrigo came out with two more boxes. He walked over to the truck and opened the back door to inspect the loaded cargo with a critical eye.

"This truck wasn't packed right! Boys, get over here and unload this thing right now!" he ordered.

"See? I told you the luggage was supposed to go in first," Ramón reprimanded his cousin.

"We are leaving in fifteen minutes, and I want this truck loaded correctly!" Rodrigo said sternly.

"I don't think all this stuff is going to fit," said Miguel.

"Make it work!" snapped his father and walked back into the house.

The two boys clumsily unloaded the truck and stood staring at the boxes and luggage piled on the concrete. It didn't seem fair to either of them that they had to do the hard work of loading the truck. They weren't included in the family's vacation plans. Once they arrived at their grandmother's house, they would be left behind while Miguel's parents and little sister drove to Santa Fe for a big family reunion. It was their punishment.

"How long did Dad say we were going to stay at Grandma's?" Miguel asked picking up a heavy piece of luggage.

"One whole month, remember?" Ramón answered.

The boys both shook their heads in disbelief that they had to spend half of their summer vacation in a remote town in northern Arizona. Neither one could imagine what they had done to deserve such a terrible fate. Miguel had to cancel a two-week soccer camp for advanced players and Ramón had to cancel his plans to spend the first part of his summer vacation with a favorite cousin in Los Angeles. When they got back home, they were not going to be allowed time with friends. Their summer was ruined.

"Let's get going!" Rodrigo yelled, closing the garage door.

Miguel's mother and little sister climbed into the SUV. The two boys followed.

"I want to sit up front!" insisted Marisol. "Miguel always pulls my braids!"

"Now, Marisol, you have to sit in a seat with a seatbelt. Get into the second seat behind me. Miguel, sit on the opposite end," ordered his mother.

"I don't want any funny business back there. We have a four-hour trip, and I have no intention of stopping for anything, but I will if I have to straighten either one of you out!" shouted Rodrigo to the boys.

Miguel and Ramón remained silent and adjusted their iPod earbuds in their ears. Four hours was a long time in the family car with nothing to do.

Marisol climbed into the back and organized her dolls and pink backpack on the spacious bench seat. As soon as she was situated she felt a tug on her braids.

"Stop it!" she screamed. "Mom, he's pulling on my hair!"

"Miguel, please don't start that now, your father needs to concentrate on his driving!" reacted the mother.

"Keep it up, boys, and you'll be walking to your grandmother's house!" yelled the father.

"Rodrigo, please," said the mother.

"Connie, let me handle this," Rodrigo replied. After thinking to himself for a moment he added, "You know, that's not a bad idea."

"What do you mean?" Connie asked, adjusting her handbag on the floorboard of the truck.

"I should have thought of it before. I should have had both boys walk to my mother's house. They could have made it in a few days," he said, half joking.

"He's just kidding, just leave your sister alone," said Connie to the boys.

"They would never make it anyway, only real men take on the impossible," Rodrigo chided.

Miguel and Ramón turned up the volume on their iPods. The thought of being abandoned in Arizona was bad enough but to have to listen to their father's belittling remarks on the way to their desert internment was excruciating.

chapter 2

"The boys will be just fine, don't you worry. I'll take good care of them," reassured Abuelita Rosa.

"Mamá, I know you will, but I want them to do all the work on this list," insisted Rodrigo, handing a piece of paper to his mother. "Everything on this list must be completed by the time we get back."

"*Ay, mijo*, there's so much to do," Abuelita Rosa said, reading the list with her tired eyes. "Maybe if they did half . . . ."

"No, Mamá. I want all of it done, no excuses!"

Abuelita Rosa didn't argue with her headstrong son. She went back to the kitchen and checked on the food cooking on the stove. When her family had arrived, they had been greeted by the warm, familiar scents of her house. A fresh pot of rice and spicy tamales were warming in the oven and the *mole* sauce needed just one more stir. She picked up the large spoon from the tiled countertop and asked her family to sit at her table.

"Boys, come and eat," said Connie.

The television was blaring in the small living room. Sounds of gunfire and explosions vibrated through the house.

"Turn that thing off and get over here!" yelled Rodrigo. "I should have never allowed you to bring a video game system. What was I thinking?"

"But it gives the boys something to do when they visit. I don't want them to be bored," Abuelita Rosa answered.

Rodrigo glared at the expensive video equipment and the stack of games lying scattered on the floor. The intrusive noise of the television had been turned off but the irritating sounds still echoed in his head.

"I don't want you two just playing video games while we're gone. You have a lot of work to do," Rodrigo warned, sitting down at the head of the kitchen table.

"They should have some fun, too. It's their summer vacation," suggested Abuelita Rosa.

"Why do they give kids vacations in the summer?" Rodrigo replied. "No one gives *me* a vacation and I work hard to support my family. I have to make my own vacations!"

"Let's have a nice dinner. Tomorrow we'll be leaving and the boys will have plenty of time to think about why they are here," said Connie.

"You're too hard on them, *mijo*. They're just boys," added Abuelita Rosa.

"Things are different now, Mamá. It's not like when Enrique and I were growing up."

Rodrigo looked at his brother's picture placed on the wood sideboard next to the kitchen table. The youthful face of his brother stood staring out at the family from the gold metal frame. Rodrigo's chest tightened with the sudden remembrance of grief, and he paused before continuing his thoughts aloud.

"These kids nowadays don't respect authority. They don't know what it takes to be real men in today's world," he lectured. "We didn't grow up with all the advantages that kids have today. I remember working every summer. We had to work for what we had."

"*Mijo,* don't you remember the special trips you made with your father and Enrique?" Abuelita Rosa asked patiently.

"If we did go on trips it's because we earned it!" Rodrigo replied without thinking.

Abuelita Rosa listened to her son with love. When the last plate of food was served on the table she said softly to Rodrigo, "Things are not so different, *mijo*. Boys still need guidance and love to grow up strong."

Rodrigo heard his mother's words and didn't contradict her, out of respect. He quietly sopped up the *mole* sauce with a warm tortilla and whispered to himself, "I know what's best for my sons."

chapter 3

The morning sun came streaming through the bedroom window and slowly awakened the slumbering boys. They stirred in their warm beds and slowly opened their eyes to the sunlight, still in the comfort of boyhood dreams.

"What do you mean they're still in bed! Do you know what time it is?!" Rodrigo's voice shouted in anger as it penetrated the walls of the bedroom. Rodrigo was already in a turbulent mood and the thought of two healthy boys sleeping through the morning hours irritated him even more.

"Marisol, go knock on the door and see if Miguel and Ramón are awake yet," Connie ordered. She was nervously packing the ice chest with contents from the refrigerator, trying not to forget anything.

Marisol finished her bowl of chocolate-flavored cereal and slowly slid off the kitchen chair. "I was up early so I could help," she reminded her father who had just sat down with a road map and a cup of coffee.

"I know, *mi preciosa*. You're my angel," he smiled in response to the little girl. He took a drink from the mug and unfolded the map to view their destination.

Marisol casually walked through the long hallway of her grandmother's house and knocked on the boys' bedroom door: "Miguel, Ramón, you better get up, or else!"

She walked back to the kitchen and grabbed a doughnut from the counter. She took a bite and gave the rest to her father.

Abuelita Rosa was busy making flour tortillas. The rolling pin glided smoothly under her rough, small hands.

She lightly floured the wood board and flipped the dough in place.

"I'll make some extra for the trip," she said, partly to herself, as the steaming, cooked tortillas piled high on a kitchen towel.

"If we travel down the interstate after passing through Flagstaff, we'll make better time," Rodrigo said to his wife, who was unpacking the ice chest to rearrange it.

"We should reach Santa Fe in three days, that's if we stop to rest and see the sights along the way. Would you like that, Marisol?" he asked.

Marisol smiled, with white-powdered sugar on her face, and nodded her head while tipping the cereal bowl to drink the chocolate-flavored milk.

"There is so much to do, Rodrigo. I hope we can leave within the hour."

Connie remembered all her husband's past warnings to his family about starting trips early in the day. After trying to reorganize the ice chest, she conceded that it wasn't large enough for the contents. The water bottles were left out along with Marisol's snack bars.

"The boys need to help us repack the car, it's the least they can do," Rodrigo said focusing his attention on the map. From the corner of his eye, he saw two figures appear in the kitchen doorway.

"Oh, thank you for blessing us with your presence, young princes," Rodrigo said in a sardonic tone.

Miguel and Ramón didn't respond to the teasing. They pulled out chairs from the kitchen table and sat down, both staring into nowhere.

"*Hijos*, what can I get you to eat? *¿Qué quieren comer?*" Abuelita Rosa asked the boys tenderly, and set a pile of fresh tortillas in the middle of the table. She also placed a plate with doughnuts and two glasses of orange juice. Rodrigo looked up from his map with a disapproving look but kept quiet.

"I don't know," answered Miguel, as he grabbed a doughnut and slid a glass of orange juice to himself. The grandmother filled two plates with eggs, beans, and *chorizo* and started to assemble a larger plate for her son.

"Mamá, just make me a burrito with a lot of *chorizo*," Rodrigo ordered from his seat.

"*Sí, mijo.*"

Abuelita Rosa quickly assembled the burrito and placed the plate in front of her son.

Taking the burrito in his hands, he took a large bite and chewed in satisfaction. With his mouth half full he said, "We have to go over the rules before we leave."

His eyes focused on his son first, then on his nephew. "See that box over there?" He pointed to an empty cardboard box sitting on the floor. "I want all of your video games, iPods, cell phones, *todas sus cosas.* You're not keeping anything here!"

The boys ate their eggs with a fork and scooped up their beans and *chorizo* with the flour tortillas. They heard the command and glanced at each other between bites.

"Can't we at least keep the video game player?" begged Miguel.

"That machine is a big waste of time, I've already unplugged it and it's getting loaded into the truck! You'll have plenty of work to keep you busy!" Rodrigo said.

After a few minutes of uncomfortable silence at the kitchen table, Ramón had the courage to speak up first. "Tío, what if there's an emergency, shouldn't we have our cell phones, at least?" The question seemed reasonable to him and he held his gaze on his uncle waiting for a rational reply.

"I don't care about your emergencies. What kind of emergencies could the two of you have?!" Rodrigo's voice rose in anger as he put down the map. "I'm facing having a son and a nephew who don't care about their futures. Who am I going to call with *my* emergency?" He grinned to himself, pleased at his artful response.

"Maybe Ramón is right," Connie said from behind the kitchen counter. "Something could happen and they may need to reach us."

"Connie, I've made a decision and they are going to follow the rules. That's it!" Rodrigo rose from the table and grabbed the box from the floor and roared, "I want all your junk in here now!"

The boys got up and went to the bedroom to retrieve the items demanded. They mournfully put their iPods, cell phones, and video games in the box, then sank back into the kitchen chairs.

"Let them finish eating, *mijo*," Abuelita Rosa requested, feeling bad for her grandsons.

"That's all they're good for, sleeping and eating. Neither one would know what to do if they were on their own. They can't even take care of themselves!" Rodrigo threw his hands up in the air and walked outside to pack the SUV.

Connie sat down at the table with the boys and drank a cup of coffee as they finished their breakfast. She looked at their young faces and remembered them as they were as young children only a few years ago. Miguel was her son. He had always been taller and rougher than the other kids but she knew he had a tender heart. Ramón was her nephew, her husband's brother's son. His dad, Enrique, had died when Ramón was only three years old. She looked at Ramón lovingly. The family had agreed to allow Rodrigo and Connie to raise Ramón after the accident. Ramón's mother had been too depressed to care for her child. Miguel and Ramón had been raised as brothers.

Connie sipped the coffee slowly and looked down to the floor at the box holding the boys' treasures. All those things had been bought to encourage them to do better in school. Rodrigo wanted the boys to have everything that he didn't have when he was growing up and Connie knew it hurt him to take these things away after giving them as gifts.

It was after the sixth grade that both boys started having trouble at school.

Both Miguel and Ramón had been involved in two fights within just the past month. No one had been seriously hurt, but the school principal wanted to expel them. When Connie and her husband met with the school guidance counselor, he said that their violent behavior was due to peer pressure and that they both needed more discipline at home. Connie remembered walking out of the counselor's office feeling embarrassed and ashamed of what they had told her and her husband. Rodrigo had gone into a rage and threatened to send each one to a military school if they didn't shape up.

They were also deeply concerned about the boys' grades. Miguel had been a good student, especially in history and science. The teachers at his middle school had told Connie that her son would be a natural as a history teacher. He especially liked the study of ancient civilizations. Rodrigo had bought him numerous books on ancient Egypt and Greece, hoping that his son would learn more than he did in school. But as the months passed, Miguel stopped reading the books and his interest in school diminished.

Ramón had never done well in school, even as a young child. His teachers had described him as not attentive in class and not focused on his assignments. The young boy was interested and talented in art and music, but the teachers and school counselors never allowed for his unique abilities. With their recent failures, Miguel and Ramón had begun to doubt themselves in school and in life.

Connie took a deep breath and finished her coffee.

Now the boys were finished with middle school and about to enter their first year in high school. Both Rodrigo and Connie wanted their sons to succeed but the pressures of the modern world seemed overwhelming. They knew that the boys were at a critical point in their lives. Rodrigo had always been a strict father but he had never taken the time to raise the children. He left all family matters to his wife. He thought that a mother could handle all the responsibilities of raising two sons as long as he worked hard and provided for the family.

Connie knew that things at home couldn't stay the same. Her husband was growing angrier every day and becoming less tolerant of the boys' bad behavior. She knew the boys needed a drastic change and that her husband needed to see the boys as young men but she felt powerless to do anything.

"I'm leaving plenty of food in the refrigerator and Abuelita Rosa will take good care of you," Connie said soothingly. She then took her wallet from the tote bag on the counter and opened it.

"Here is $100 in case you need money. Miguel, put it in your pocket before your father comes back."

Miguel took the five twenty-dollar bills and put them in his front pocket quickly when he heard his father open the door.

"The car's packed and started. Let's get going." Rodrigo had packed the SUV himself, in spite of his earlier demands that the boys help. He picked up the box filled with the boys' belongings and took one last look at them.

"I don't want to hear anything from either of you while we are gone, and don't expect phone calls from us. We'll call before we start heading back home."

With those last words to the boys, Rodrigo kissed his mother on the cheek and motioned for his wife to follow him out to the waiting car.

Connie kissed Miguel and Ramón on their foreheads, "We'll be back soon, we love you," she said.

Marisol was packing her pink backpack in the living room while listening to the conversation from the kitchen. She stuffed one last DVD into the side pocket and ran to her grandmother for a hug goodbye.

She looked at the boys as she readjusted her jacket and braids and said, "I'm going to have fun at Tio's party, I'll ride horses, swim, everything, and you're going to be stuck here in the middle of nowhere!" She laughed, picked up her backpack, and lifted her nose in the air as she skipped to the car.

Manuel and Ramón slumped in their seats and glanced out the kitchen window as their family drove off for a summer vacation without them.

chapter 4

The morning air was warm and dry. June was always a hot but tolerable month in northern Arizona. The trees along the side of the house provided shade for the side yard and some of the backyard as well. The old shed was located behind the house alongside the carport. It was a weather-worn shade of green and, despite the lack of water, small weeds were accumulating in the dirt along the walls. The door to the shed was bolted shut with a lock and looked as if it hadn't been opened in years.

"Are you sure this is on the list?" Miguel asked, shaking the lock, then wiping his hands on his pants.

"Yeah, it is." Ramón took the list out of his back pocket and read the fateful words aloud to his cousin: "Organize the shed contents in a manner which behooves a decent individual."

"What does that mean?" Miguel asked.

"It means, no fooling around, we have to empty this thing out."

The boys looked down the list to see if there was another chore to do that was less disagreeable. To the boys' horror, the list included washing windows and screens, repainting the side of the car port, scrubbing the two bathrooms, and clearing the yard of weeds. After carefully evaluating the list, they decided that the shed was not as bad as the other awful chores. They unlocked the shed door in dreaded anticipation of what it held inside.

The shed was packed to the ceiling with junk.

"You've got to be kidding me," Miguel said with a moan.

"This is no joke." Ramón stared into the shed and put on his work gloves, motioning for Miguel to do the same. "We better get started. I'll pull out the stuff on the top and hand it to you to put over there." Ramón pointed to the open grassy area that was a few feet away.

The morning hours passed as the boys slowly unraveled and untangled all the contents of the shed. Piece by piece each object was pulled out. Rusty metal objects, sports equipment, and Christmas decorations made big piles on the lawn.

"What are we going to do with this junk when we pull it all out?" questioned Miguel, exhausted from the lifting.

"Abuelita Rosa said she was going to call someone at her church to pick it up so they can sell it for charity," Ramón answered, while pulling out items from the entrance of the shed.

Underneath stacks of old blankets wrapped in plastic bags was an object that looked promising. Ramón carefully lifted the plastic bundles and moved the golf clubs from the floor around the newfound treasure.

"Hey, Miguel, I think I found something here!" said Ramón. He slowly pulled the object out of the shed onto the grass.

"No way. What is that?" Miguel stood over the two-wheel contraption covered with spiderwebs and dust.

"It's a Vespa!"

Ramón's eyes were wide with excitement, and he grabbed an old towel and began to wipe away the spiderwebs.

"Does it run?"

"Who knows, but maybe . . . " replied Ramón.

The motor scooter leaned on its sturdy metal stand and resonated with adventures of a bygone youth. The blue paint was still smooth and the metal framework had not rusted despite years of neglect. The seat was made of black leather and had enough room for two. A small luggage rack was fitted on the back of the seat and the two tires were worn slightly but still in good condition.

"It's a sign from God!" said Ramón, reverently inspired by the new treasure.

"You're crazy," Miguel laughed. "It's a sign we have more work to do."

Miguel went back to the shed and began to remove more useless objects.

"No, seriously, if we can get this thing to run, we have transportation for the summer!"

"What's the use of transportation? We have no where to go. Remember where we are?" Miguel pointed to the dirt road leading out onto a desolate street. "There's nothing out here, man."

Ramón didn't hear Miguel's negative words. He kept cleaning off the scooter and dreaming of an open road leading to somewhere.

chapter 5

The kitchen smelled of roasted chicken and *mole*. Abuelita Rosa was a great cook and nothing made her happier than to feed her darling grandsons. They had often spent the summer with her and their grandfather, Esteban, while he had been alive. Abuelita Rosa reflected on those summer days when Esteban would take the boys on fishing and camping trips in the mountains. She missed her husband but looking after her grandsons kept her mind busy.

Squeezing the lime juice into the fresh salsa she thought about how Enrique's features were in the face of Ramón. He resembled his father more as the days passed.

"*Mi pobre hijo*, he was so young to die."

Tears came to her eyes for a moment, then she shook her head and remembered not to cry. She still had a lifetime to cry, but for the moment she had to fix dinner for her hungry grandsons.

That evening, the three family members sat at the kitchen table. The boys ate hungrily. They swallowed glasses of sweet iced tea and sopped up all the *mole* sauce off their plates with tortillas.

"I don't want you to work so hard tomorrow," Abuelita Rosa said, looking with pity at the tired boys. "You don't have to do all that work right away. I want you to have fun, too." She realized that her small town wasn't interesting for boys their age and felt sorry for them. They would have to spend four weeks doing nothing but chores.

"It's okay, Abuelita," said Miguel. "The work will keep us busy. Besides, my dad took all our stuff anyway."

Ramón nodded in agreement as he stuffed his mouth with one more helping of chicken.

"Well, we still have the television. You know that I go to bed early so you'll have the living room to yourselves every night," she consoled them.

Both boys considered the thought. The television only received local channels, six to be exact. It was hardly something to get excited about.

The boys helped clear the dishes then plopped onto the sofa to watch the local news program, hoping that an old movie might be on later.

"Grandma, do you have a VCR or DVD player?" Ramón asked.

"*Sí, mijo*, I have one in my bedroom. You can connect it to the living room television, I never use it."

Ramón raised his eyebrows in surprise and thought that maybe the situation wasn't completely hopeless. Then he considered the fact that the nearest video rental store was two miles down the road. He reconciled the matter with the happy thought of the scooter. Maybe that would be its purpose for the summer.

"Goodnight, Abuelita," the boys said in unison staring at the local weather report on the television.

"*Buenas noches*," Abuelita Rosa replied, walking slowly to her bedroom.

Miguel and Ramón stayed on the sofa and stared at the television for the rest of the night.

chapter 6

The next morning, the boys awoke to a quiet house. The sun was shining brightly into the bedroom window.

"Hey, what time is it?" Miguel asked, looking with half-closed eyes at his cousin.

"What, what are you talking about?"

Ramón was still trying to sleep.

"It's almost ten o'clock, man," Miguel suddenly realized.

"So what?" Ramón said in an agitated voice.

Miguel turned on his back and stared up at the ceiling. The house was really quiet. He thought to himself that by that time the house always smelled of food. They should have heard their grandmother's footsteps down the hall.

"Hey, we should get up. This is weird," Miguel said, sitting up in bed.

"Whatever."

Ramón then opened his eyes, remembering the scooter on the lawn outside and the leftover chicken *mole*. "Yeah, I guess we should get up."

They both put on their jeans and T-shirts from the folded stacks left for them on the dresser. They opened the door and walked out to the hall. The house was still. No one was walking about or cooking in the kitchen.

"Where's Abuelita?" Miguel said, remembering all the years that he had awoken to his grandmother cooking in the kitchen.

"Check in her bedroom," Ramón suggested.

"Come with me."

Miguel gave Ramón a commanding look and they both walked toward their grandmother's bedroom door. The door was unlocked and opened with a small squeak.

"Abuelita, are you awake?" Miguel whispered.

No one answered. Their grandmother was in her bed facing away from the door. A soft peach quilt covered her small, still body.

In a louder voice, Ramón asked, "Abuelita, are you okay?"

She didn't answer. The boys crept closer to the bed, softly touched her shoulder and shook it gently.

"Abuelita, wake up, wake up!"

Abuelita Rosa did not wake up.

chapter 7

buelita Rosa was breathing but her breath was slow and shallow. Miguel carefully turned her over onto her back and felt for a pulse, holding her wrist gently in his hand.

"I think I feel a pulse, but I'm not sure," he said, feeling his own heart pounding.

Ramón was nervously pacing the room and his eyes darted from the bed to the telephone on the bedside table. He quickly grabbed the phone and dialed 911.

"Hello? Yeah, my grandmother is in bed and I don't think she's doing well. I-I mean . . . I-I think something is wrong," he stammered. "I don't know what's wrong. Shouldn't you send somebody over here or something?" His voice grew impatient and rose with his next response, "Just send somebody over here. I don't know what's wrong!"

Meanwhile Miguel was gently patting his grandma's hands and speaking softly to her, "It'll be okay, Abuelita. Somebody's coming over here to check on you, just stay still and rest."

His words were calm but Miguel knew deep inside that something was terribly wrong. His grandmother had always taken medication for various ailments for as long as he could remember but he had never seen her unconscious before.

"When are they coming?" Miguel asked anxiously.

Ramón had just hung up the phone.

"They said they will send someone over right away."

Ramón kept pacing, looking about the dark bedroom nervously. He went to the windows and drew back the curtains, allowing the sunlight to enter the room. Only two or three minutes had passed since they had first seen her lying still, but it felt like hours.

"Ramón, get her medications and put them in a plastic bag to give to the paramedics. I saw that on a TV commercial; you're supposed to do that when an old person goes to the hospital." Miguel ordered.

"Good idea," answered Ramón and ran to the kitchen. He grabbed a large plastic bag from a drawer and went in search of the prescription bottles he had seen next to the sink. Six bottles went into the plastic bag along with a few pharmacy receipts he saw stacked in a corner on the kitchen counter.

"Okay, I got them," he announced, running back.

"Put that bag down, get Abuelita's purse and her suitcase from the closet. Put some of her stuff in there," Miguel directed from the bedside.

"What stuff?"

"I don't know. Go into the bathroom and pack her lotions, toothbrush, stuff like that . . . " Then he added, after pausing, "also two or three nightgowns."

As Miguel thought of which of his grandmother's belongings should be packed, he remembered being rushed to the hospital as a small child many times when an asthma attack would strike. His grandmother never left his bedside and she always brought his toys to the hospital even when the nurses told her not to.

The ambulance finally arrived. Ramón ran outside to meet it and led the paramedics through the house to his grandmother's bedroom.

"All right boys, step aside," the paramedic ordered. "We can handle this now."

Miguel and Ramón took a few steps back and watched the paramedics use a black armband to check their grandmother's blood pressure and a stethoscope to listen to her heart.

"Is she going to be okay?" Miguel asked, trying to look over the shoulder of one of the paramedics.

"We don't know yet. Please step back," the young man replied curtly.

Miguel and Ramón held their breaths as the emergency examination continued. After a few moments, the paramedics arranged the gurney and started to prepare their grandmother to be lifted onto it.

"Are you going to take her to the hospital?" Miguel asked with fear in his voice.

"Yes, she has to go. She needs more tests."

"Here, take this," Miguel grabbed the plastic bag with her prescription, her purse, and the small suitcase. "She might need these."

"Are you kids all alone?" asked one of the paramedics.

"No, my mom will be right back," Miguel lied.

Their grandmother was moved onto the gurney and wheeled out of the bedroom. The boys followed the paramedics outside and watched their grandmother disappear through the red-and-white doors. The ambulance drove away with the lights twirling and the sirens blasting.

chapter 8

Miguel and Ramón sat at the kitchen table in silence. The morning was nearly gone and in the span of only a few hours their lives had changed forever. The house was unbearably quiet, with the occasional noise of passing cars in the distance. The day held no promise.

"Do you think we should call my dad?" Miguel asked in a low voice.

"We cannot make long-distance calls from Abuelita's phone. Remember that he took our phones? He doesn't want us to call them," Ramón replied, looking at the useless black phone mounted on the wall.

"Yeah, but this is an emergency!"

"Remember what he said about emergencies?"

"Yeah, I remember." Miguel slouched in the kitchen chair and thought about the hunger pangs in his stomach. "I'm going to make a burrito, you want one?"

"Yeah, make me one without *chorizo*."

Miguel walked to the refrigerator and pulled out the containers filled with beans, rice, and *chorizo*. He placed the cast-iron grill pan on the stove and warmed up the flour tortillas. The smells of the warming food made him think of his grandmother and tears began to fill his eyes.

"What if she dies?" his voice cracked as he spoke.

"Don't say that!" Ramón yelled out. "Don't be negative!"

"Yeah, but what if she's really sick?"

"We have to be positive." Ramón thought for a moment, then added, "We have to call Tío Rodrigo, he doesn't know what happened."

Miguel hadn't considered the possibility that his father wouldn't know about their grandmother's sudden illness. "Doesn't the hospital have phone numbers to call when someone gets sick?"

"I think so, but we should call anyway. We can use the phone at the gas station. Let's go after we eat."

The boys ate their burritos quickly and didn't say another word. Although each one was thinking of their grandmother and the grim possibility of her death, neither boy wanted to face losing her.

The distance from the house to the nearest gas station was a mile. The boys walked at a fast pace and within minutes arrived at the dusty and vacant establishment.

"Is anyone here?" Miguel asked, looking around at the empty spaces between the gas pumps.

"Probably inside the store. I'll go look." Ramón walked around the side of a small building and entered through an open door. The attendant was sitting behind a crowded counter filled with beef jerky, candy, and assorted key fobs.

"Hey, do you have a pay phone around here?" Ramón asked.

The attendant was slightly older than Ramón and barely noticed anyone walking in.

"No, the phone was taken out a long time ago." He continued to read his magazine and never looked up again.

"Where can we find a pay phone? We really need to call someone."

"I don't know. I think there's one outside the market about a mile or so down the road," replied the disinterested clerk.

Ramón told Miguel the bad news. "Can you believe this, another mile!"

"Well, let's go," Miguel replied.

The boys walked down the road at a slower pace and eventually found a pay phone

"Okay, you call your dad and tell him." Ramón took the quarters from his pocket and gave them to Miguel.

"Why can't you call him?"

"He's your dad. If I call him, he'll get mad," Ramón answered.

"He'll get mad if *I* call him!"

The boys looked at each other, wondering what to do next. Then Ramón came up with a brilliant idea: "Let's flip for it. Heads, you call; tails, I call."

The quarter flipped in the air and landed on the dusty ground below. Miguel had to make the fateful call. He put the coins in the slot and dialed his dad's cell-phone number.

The phone rang and rang with no answer, then the message began: "This is Rodrigo, I can't take your call right now; please leave a message. I'll be on vacation for the next month, so I may not receive your message. Please call my office if this call is business-related."

"There's no answer. It says to call his office," Miguel repeated.

Miguel dialed the number to his father's office and a friendly voice answered.

"May I help you?"

"Hi, this is Miguel, Rodrigo's son, can I leave a message? It's important."

"Sure, no problem. Can you hold?"

"Yeah."

"What did they say?" asked Ramón impatiently.

"I'm on hold."

"Okay, this message is for who?" the voice continued.

"My dad, Rodrigo."

"You must be Miguel!" the voice said enthusiastically.

"Yeah, can I leave a message?"

"Go right ahead. Oh, wait a minute, I have to put you on hold again."

Miguel stared at the ground and waited for the voice to come back.

"Okay, go ahead."

"Could you tell him, that my grandma's sick in the hospital and that me and Ramón are at the house alone?"

"Oh, how terrible, is your grandma okay?" the voice asked.

"I don't know. Would you give him that message right away?"

"Tell them to tell your dad to call home!" Ramón interjected.

"Oh, yeah, could you tell him to call home?" Miguel added quickly.

"Does he have the number—oh, of course he does," the voice replied absent-mindedly. "I'll give him the message as soon as he calls in."

"It's really important that he gets the message."

"I'll make sure he does" the voice reassured. "I have to go, there's another call waiting."

Miguel hung up the phone.

"What are we gonna to do?" asked Ramón.

"I don't know," replied Miguel. "I guess we better head back and wait for Dad to call."

The boys walked in the direction of their grandmother's house, occasionally stepping off the side of the road to kick a rock or pick up an interesting stick. There wasn't a rush to get home. There was nothing but chores waiting for them. The cars drove by anonymously.

chapter 9

"There's nothing on TV," complained Miguel.

The boys were back at their grandmother's house, sitting in front of the small screen, thinking about what to do for the rest of the day.

"Maybe we should call the hospital and see how Abuelita's doing."

"Yeah, get the phone book."

Ramón found the phone number for the local hospital and dialed the number.

"Are you over eighteen?" asked the patronizing voice on the other side of the phone line.

"No, I'm her grandson. My cousin and me were with her when she got sick."

"Well, we can't give out any information about her condition unless you're an adult and her nearest relation. It's for her protection."

"Can we see her?"

"Well, I don't know who 'we' is, but if you're under eighteen years of age, you may not enter her hospital room without an adult."

"How long is she going to be in the hospital?"

"At least the rest of the week, but I can't give you any more information than that."

Ramón hung up the phone and sat quietly next to Miguel on the sofa. The television was blaring with images of a new super-speed household appliance that the salesperson was trying to sell, "And for a limited time . . . ."

"Hey, man, what are we gonna do? We can't sit here for a month without money, no phone, nothing. And what if my dad never calls?" said Miguel facing the television.

"Let me think." Ramón tuned out the noise in the room and put his mind to thinking up a solution to their problem.

Ramón first considered the possibility of the two of them surviving in the house by themselves. They had a little money to buy groceries and after four weeks their family would return. And maybe, he thought, their grandmother wasn't that sick, maybe she would be home in a day or two and everything would be okay. But then he considered the possibility of their grandmother not returning home. Four weeks was a long time to be alone in the remote house. His mind twisted and turned over their dilemma.

The television channel was tuned to a sitcom rerun and the canned audience laughter filled the room.

"Hey, turn that down, I've got it!" Ramón said suddenly, rising from the sofa with excitement.

"What's the plan?" Miguel asked eagerly.

Ever since they were small boys Ramón had always been the planner in their adventures and Miguel never ceased to be impressed with his cousin's ingenuity to solve a problem, no matter how difficult it was.

"Okay." Ramón took a deep breath. "Listen to the whole thing before you say anything, all right?"

"Yeah, yeah, go on!"

"All right, this is the plan. We can't stay here, that's for sure. For one thing, Tío Rodrigo will be really mad if he finds out we were by ourselves without adult supervision, right?" Ramón asked, waiting for an affirmative nod from his cousin.

Miguel nodded and listened for the rest of the solution.

"Remember that scooter we found in the shed? Well, we're gonna drive it to Santa Fe!"

"What? Are you crazy?"

"No, man, listen, that scooter probably goes around 40 to 50 miles per hour. If we can drive six hours a day we'll get there in three or four days. We might even catch up with them along the road, wouldn't that be awesome?"

"I don't know, Ramón. Does that scooter even run?"

"Well, we'll have to work on that. I'm going outside to start. Meanwhile gather up all the money you can find; the gas won't be free."

"What about food? Where will we sleep?"

"We probably won't be on the road more than three days. We have our sleeping bags and we can pack some food too. We'll make it work!"

"You sound like my dad!"

"Well, it's the only idea I can think of!" answered Ramón. "I know it sounds impossible, but if we believe we can do it, we can!" he added.

"I don't know, Ramón. What about Abuelita? We can't just leave her."

"We're gonna go to the hospital to see her first and tell her where we're going," Ramón replied.

"But they won't let us in!"

"Leave that to me," Ramón said with confidence. "You start thinking about what we need to take and I'll go check on our ride!"

Miguel stood in the middle of the living room and considered the crazy plan he had just heard. They would have to travel hundreds of miles and camp out alone in the wilderness with little money and hardly any food. The task seemed insurmountable. They had never been on such a crazy adventure before, but maybe it was the right thing to do, maybe it was time.

chapter 10

The scooter leaned on the grass among the discarded Christmas decorations and old sports equipment. Ramón moved the shed's former contents to one side of the yard and rolled the scooter away from the pile.

He decided he would fill the gas tank and try to start the scooter first before checking the other parts. Along the side of the carport, his uncle always kept a container of gasoline for emergencies. He filled the tank with the gas and sealed it. "Well," he thought, "here goes nothing." He pressed the button for the electronic ignition and nothing happened. Disappointed but not discouraged, he ran back into the house to tell his cousin that he was leaving.

"Miguel, I have to take the Vespa to the gas station and see if I can work on it there," he said with confidence.

"Okay," said Miguel, momentarily distracted by his task. Seconds later he added, "I'll start getting our stuff ready while you're gone. Where are the sleeping bags?"

Ramón was already walking toward the road with the scooter when he turned around and shouted back to his cousin. "Look in the closet in the bedroom we were sleeping in! Make sure they're rolled up real tight to save space. Remember how Grandpa showed us?"

Miguel ran to the closet, making a mental list of what they should take on the trip. He grabbed a pad of paper and a pen from a kitchen drawer and started to murmur to himself as he wrote. "Okay, sleeping bags, backpacks . . . " He stopped for a second and remembered that they didn't have their iPods. "Well, no music for now. We need food, water, matches, a flashlight, a knife, and a few T-shirts. We'll only be on the road for three days. We should be all right."

He carried his list through the house and began to gather the items. The matches, flashlight, and knife were no problem to find, but he wasn't sure what type of food they should take with them. He remembered his grandfather packing for their camping trips. He always told them not to eat food that had spoiled.

Miguel opened the refrigerator and looked at the contents. All the good food was in containers and would probably spoil within a few hours in the heat. He looked longingly at the containers of *chorizo* and *mole*, there was no way they could take that. "We'll just have to eat a lot before we go," he thought. He took out the rice and beans and tortillas and within a few minutes he had rolled six burritos in tinfoil. Next he looked in the pantry for canned goods to take. He grabbed a few granola bars, a pack of peanuts, and two chocolate bars.

Bottled water was heavy to carry so he decided to take only eight small bottles, four in each backpack. Miguel wrapped the food items in plastic bags and stored them in the refrigerator.

The sleeping bags were larger than what he had remembered. "Oh, no, how will these fit on the back of that scooter?" he asked himself, remembering the small luggage rack on the back of the seat. He took one sleeping bag and laid it out flat on the floor, then with all his skill he rolled it up to one-half the size that it had been before.

"We can only take one sleeping bag, so I guess we'll have to take turns sleeping in it," he resolved. The solution of trading off nights seemed reasonable to Miguel, especially if they were planning only two nights outside.

Both boys had brought backpacks with them. Miguel took his and emptied out all the stuff inside to make room for the necessities of the trip. The video games were worthless without the machine to play them on, and his soccer shoes came out too. Only the essentials remained.

Ramón had been walking slower than he had earlier in the day. The scooter was much heavier than a bicycle to push and the deflated tires caused it to drag as he steered it along his right side. He had stuffed a screwdriver and a wrench into his jean pockets. He hoped he could fix the Vespa with the limited tools he had. "I'll be glad when I can ride it home," he thought with optimism.

He rolled the scooter up to the air hose and put a quarter in the canister.

chapter 11

When Ramón attached the air compressor nozzle to the rubber inner tubes of the tires nothing happened. The air compressor made a lot of noise and the tires did nothing but make a hissing sound. He stood back in disappointment and wondered what to do next. Then he got the idea of cleaning the small engine with baking soda. He had seen his uncle Rodrigo clean an old lawn mower last summer using the strange homemade cleaner. He went inside the convenience store to buy the items needed.

"Hey, do you have baking soda and a bowl or something I could use?" he asked the attendant.

The nineteen-year-old glared at the younger boy and was visibly irritated at having to reply to his request.

"Check on the last aisle on the bottom shelf," he said without enthusiasm.

Ramón found the small box he was looking for and grabbed a shallow paper bowl from the food counter. The bowl was intended for a serving of nachos, but he thought it would work for the job he had in mind. He then picked up a toothbrush and took his purchase to the counter.

"There's water by the air compressor," the clerk said, taking the money from the young boy.

Ramón was surprised at this. He didn't think the clerk had noticed what he had been doing. He paid for the items and went outside to start his project. He took out the rusted spark plug from the small engine, using his wrench, and began cleaning it with the baking soda solution. After reinstalling the old spark plug he attempted to start the engine again and to his dread, nothing happened.

"You probably need new spark plug wire," said a voice from around the gas pump.

Ramón looked up with a discouraged look on his face and saw an older man holding a large paper cup of coffee and a doughnut wrapped in wax paper. The old man took a big bite of the sugary treat and stared directly at the blue scooter with interest.

"Looks like it's been out of commission for a few years," he said in a good-natured tone.

"Yeah, me and my cousin found it at my grandma's house," Ramón said flatly. "We were going to drive it to Sante Fe but I can't get it started."

"Is that right?" the old man said, surprised upon hearing the bold plans. "That's quite a distance, but I guess if you drive straight through on the interstate you could probably make good time," he said, scratching his head. "I've made the trip plenty of times myself. I guess a bike like that could work. 'Sometimes you got to grab the bull by the horns,' that's what my old friend Esteban used to say," he added. "Aren't you Esteban's kid? He used to take you and another kid on camping trips then come back full of stories to tell!" the gray-haired man said, happy to think of his old friend again.

"Well, actually, he's our grandfather. I'm Ramón and Miguel is my cousin," he answered, surprised that the stranger knew his family.

The old man gazed off into the distance and took a long sip of his coffee. He reveled in the memories of his bygone youth and of the friends that had meant so much to him. Road trips through the desert and beyond had been a favorite pastime. He stood for a moment and recollected his first adventure driving through Arizona en route to Santa Fe.

When he looked again at Ramón's face, the disappointment was noticeable in the young boy's eyes. It was clear to the man that the boys wouldn't have their chance of taking an exciting trip without the motor scooter and he remembered Esteban always talking about how he wanted his grandsons to see the world and not be afraid of life. This persuaded the older man to help.

"Why don't you bring that bike over to my shop, and I'll see what I can do to get it running again."

"Really?" Ramón exclaimed.

"Yeah, I'll get you going on your trip. Your grandpa would have wanted me to!"

The old man finished his doughnut and coffee as he walked along the dusty road with the young boy past the gas station toward an auto-parts yard. The shop front was partially hidden behind mountains of discarded old vehicles. A wire cyclone fence surrounded the property and a large metal sign hung over the doorway of the large building. The once-bright paint had faded in the desert sun but the words were still visible, "Frank's Auto Parts and Sales."

"Yeah, me and your grandpa used to hang out here on the weekends. I'd be wheeling and dealing salvaged cars and used parts, and Esteban would be telling stories about you kids and making us all laugh. He was quite a character, your grandfather."

Ramón looked around the cluttered yard filled with half-dissected old cars and trucks parked in every direction with no apparent value other than to fill space. He rolled the scooter up to the front porch and leaned it on the kick-stand.

"Wait here. I think I have a manual for a bike like this one." The old man squinted and looked at the blue metal frame for identification. "Yeah, that's what I thought, a Vespa P200E. Well, I'll tell you, you don't find too many of these around here, but Esteban was an original," he laughed.

Ramón looked at his prized possession with renewed hope. He wanted more than anything for the scooter to be restored to running condition and he felt lucky that his grandfather's friend was willing to help out. He heard the sound of drawers opening and shutting, then the shuffling of stacks of papers coming from inside the building. While he waited for the shop owner to return, he took a few steps to look around the junkyard and felt his foot hit something soft on the ground. Looking down he was startled to see a huge tan-colored dog lying on his side with his eyes closed.

"Oh, don't mind Oscar. He's harmless. But back in the day he was a ferocious watchdog. No one dared to come onto this property without clearing it with him first!" Frank said with pride, stepping out of the doorway with the promised document.

Ramón looked again at the inanimate creature sleeping lazily on the concrete. He couldn't imagine Oscar attacking anyone in his present state.

"Well, wouldn't you believe it, I have a manual for your scooter. It's not for the exact model but it's close enough," the old man said proudly, holding up several tattered pages. "I keep everything I come across. In this business you never know when you might need something! Just the other day, a passerby asked for an exhaust pipe for his 1955 Cadillac and lo and behold I rummaged around this place and found one in mint condition. By golly, he was impressed!"

Ramón nodded his head in agreement at the man's story and readily believed it.

"Well, let's see, we can change the oil, and I might have new inner tubes for the tires. The tread still looks okay," Frank said, reviewing the tattered manual quickly. "Why don't you take out the spark plug again and remove the tires from the rims and I'll go get the parts."

Ramón found an old blanket tucked underneath a pile of boxes and spread it out on the concrete. Carefully leaning the scooter over on its side, he placed it on the blanket and began to remove the parts as instructed. Frank returned with his arms full of wires, rubber tubing, a small battery, various hand tools, and a container of motor oil.

"This isn't the exact match, it's actually for motorcycle engines, but it will have to do. Different viscosity, you understand," Frank said, placing the motor oil on the ground.

"Have you worked on motorcycles too?" Ramón asked, impressed with the old man's knowledge.

"Oh, yeah," he said letting out a big breath, "I've worked on engines of all types, even had my hand in body work early on, but the real money is in salvaged parts. You wouldn't believe it but this place is a gold mine!"

The young boy's eyes grew big, wondering if the piles of junk he saw had any value.

Oscar, invigorated by the lively conversation, picked himself up slowly and sauntered over to the two mechanics. He dropped his heavy body to the ground and rolled over on his back so that Ramón could scratch his enormous belly.

"Esteban always said, 'Frank, don't underestimate the need for specialists, even in the junk trade'," Frank smiled. "Your granddad was a smart man."

Ramón petted the contented beast lying next to him. He was happy to hear stories about his grandfather while working on the scooter. It made him feel closer to him somehow.

"Do you think we can really get it running?" Ramón asked. His excitement was growing with every turn of the wrench.

Frank worked quickly and despite his large hands he could manipulate the smallest parts of the engine.

"Yeah, we almost got it. Let's drain the oil, then we'll fill up her tires and try her out!"

"You keep saying 'she,' why is that?" Ramón questioned.

Frank paused, then answered, "Well, I guess it's because we always have. The Romans started it. Their warships were named after women and throughout history we've kept the tradition. Didn't your grandpa used to call that old truck of his Betty Lou?"

Ramón laughed loudly and replied that he had never heard his grandfather use that name before.

After the last of the repairs, they stood the scooter up on its stand. Frank finished filling the newly installed inner tubes with air. Ramón eagerly waited for the old man's signal, then he started the ignition. To his delight, the engine turned over and the bike trembled with new life.

"I can't believe it! We did it! We got it running!"

Frank smiled broadly, making the deep creases in his face even deeper. "See, kid, anything is possible. You just have to try! Keep the engine running for a while when you get home to make sure she doesn't need anything else," Frank cautioned.

"Here, I don't know how much the parts were," Ramón said, reaching into his back pocket for money.

"Don't worry about it, kid. Anything for my old friend Esteban. He'd be real proud of you and your cousin taking a trip on your own. It shows initiative. He always wanted the best for you two," Frank said.

"Thanks for everything," Ramón said.

"If you run into any trouble on the road, you just call me and I'll be there to help you," he offered, pointing to a flatbed tow truck parked off in the distance. "Yeah, me and Oscar will be there in a jiffy if you need us!"

As a last gesture of friendship, Frank took a crisp fifty dollar bill and a worn business card from his wallet. "Take this, you might need something extra on the road."

The scooter hummed impatiently as Ramón said goodbye to Oscar then to his new friend Frank. He boarded the blue machine and drove back to his grandmother's house with the happy news. The old man waved goodbye from the road.

chapter 12

The road raced by and within minutes Ramón was driving into the driveway of the house. Miguel came running out to see the scooter which by now was running smoothly.

"Ain't she great!" beamed Ramón as he climbed off the seat, careful to keep the motor running.

"I can't believe you got it started!" Miguel said in amazement, and quickly added, "She? Why does it have to be a girl?"

"All great vehicles have the names of girls, even ships back in Roman times," Ramón answered, remembering Frank's words.

"Oh, well. Should we give her a real name then?"

"Yeah, like what?" Ramón liked the idea of a nickname for his new toy.

"How about Ramona, after you?" Miguel laughed and took a step back just in case his cousin wanted to take a playful swing at him.

Ramón laughed and saw that his cousin was too far to punch on the arm.

"A real name, Miguel. She's going to take us across two states. She deserves it."

"How about the Pequod? That was the name of a ship."

"The Pequod sunk in the middle of the ocean, and everybody died!" reminded Ramón. "And Pequod sounds weird," he added after considering the name further.

"Okay, how about Natalie, after that girl you used to like in the sixth grade?"

"Natalie, yeah she was really pretty, but she didn't like me back," said Ramón with a sour look on his face.

"Well, this Natalie will love you," Miguel teased.

Ramón nodded and smiled remembering the pretty blonde in sixth grade. "Maybe she did like me a little," he thought to himself. "She did sit next to me at a soccer game once." With that happy memory, he followed his cousin inside to take inventory of the supplies for the trip.

Water bottles and other items on Miguel's list were on the kitchen counter except for the food in the refrigerator.

Ramón looked on the kitchen floor and saw one sleeping bag rolled tightly and the two backpacks on the kitchen table. "Where's the other sleeping bag?" he asked, looking around.

"I figured we can only carry one, so we'll have to share," Miguel said confidently.

"How do you share a sleeping bag?"

"We'll take turns!"

"We'll what?"

"Yeah, one night I'll sleep in it, and the next night you will," suggested Miguel. "Besides we'll only need it for two nights, right?"

Ramón considered the logic and decided the scooter could only handle one sleeping bag regardless of their desired sleeping arrangements. "Okay, forget about that. Let's go. Where's the map?"

"What map?"

"We have to have a map. How are we going to find Santa Fe?" Ramón questioned.

Miguel felt embarrassed that he hadn't thought of a map, so he tried to cover it up, "I couldn't find one. We can get one at the gas station for free when we leave."

"Yeah, that's true," Ramón replied. "How about food?"

"I've wrapped up some burritos and snacks in the refrigerator. I just need to pack them."

"Well, looks like we're ready!" Ramón's eyes lit up and he paced around the room once before settling in one of the kitchen chairs. "When should we leave?"

"We have to go to the hospital. We'll see Abuelita today and leave tomorrow in the morning," Miguel suggested.

"You're right, we'll start off tomorrow. We should eat a lot in the morning just in case our food runs out."

Miguel's face changed from excitement to dread at the thought of the food running out. "Do you think we could starve to death before we reach Santa Fe?"

Ramón considered the problem carefully. They had very little money, and a questionable mode of transportation.

"Miguel, sometimes you just got to hit the road and see what happens, you know? Take the bull by the horns! We'll be okay, we got each other."

chapter 13

"So, how are we going to get to the hospital?" questioned Miguel.

It was late in the afternoon and the concentration that Miguel had used to pack for their trip had tired him out. He could not think of another new idea.

"The Vespa, of course," Ramón answered.

"What if they don't let us in?"

"We have to act like we know what we're doing. Everyone thinks you look older anyway, just pretend that you are."

Miguel trusted his cousin's words. Since he was five years old, he could remember adults commenting on his height and asking his parents if he was much older than he was. Now at fourteen, he could easily pass for sixteen.

The boys went outside and stared at the motor scooter. Suddenly, they realized that they would have to drive on an open road for the first time. Ramón felt the most daring and spoke up first.

"Okay, get on. Let's go."

Miguel obeyed and threw his right leg over the seat. Ramón boarded last and started the motor.

"All right, Natalie, here we go!" Ramón said.

The scooter lunged forward and roared down the driveway. Miguel didn't expect the sudden bolt and his larger body shifted back off the seat. With the first jolt, Miguel slid off the scooter and tumbled down onto the asphalt driveway. Ramón didn't stay on the scooter much longer. Miguel's fall had tipped the scooter off balance and soon both boys were sprawled on the ground.

"Are you okay?" Ramón asked as he got up and ran after the scooter.

"Old Nat's got a lot of power. I wasn't expecting it. We better take it easy," said Miguel, jumping on board again.

Ramón turned the hand gears and the scooter lurched forward again. This time Miguel was ready. He was holding onto the sides of the small luggage rack and leaning his body weight forward.

"We'll get the hang of this," Ramón said, picking up speed. "Hold on!" he shouted back to his cousin.

The hospital was three miles away from their grandmother's house. The small-town streets were quiet and only a few passing cars drove by. Miguel managed to stay aboard the motor scooter while Ramón drove cautiously on the side of the road. When they arrived at the front of the entrance to the hospital, Ramón reminded his cousin how to act.

"Remember, act like you're over eighteen!"

"Eighteen! They'll know I'm not that old!"

"Lower your voice," Ramón warned. "Just act like you are. I'll do the talking when we get in."

Miguel nodded and followed his cousin through the glass double doors. The nurse's station was located in the middle of the large entry. A woman stood behind the tall countertop, dressed in a white smock and wearing wire-rimmed bifocal glasses. Looking up from her charts, she noticed the two boys as soon as they walked in.

Ramón walked up to the counter with confidence and asked where his grandmother's room was. Miguel stood to his side and tried to have an adult look on his face.

The nurse adjusted her glasses on her small nose and squinted her eyes first at Ramón then at Miguel. She pursed her thin lips tightly in an attempt to ascertain their credibility, then she spoke.

"Who are you here to see?"

"My grandmother. She came in yesterday in an ambulance," answered Ramón.

The nurse stared into Ramón's eyes for any signs of mischievousness. She then turned her hard glare at Miguel, "And who are you?"

"I'm his older brother" Miguel said nervously.

"Are your parents here?" the woman further interrogated.

"Yeah, they called us to come and visit," Ramón quickly replied.

The nurse twisted her thin lips and was preparing to tell the boys that they had to leave unless they could prove that they were accompanied by an adult when a voice announced through the hospital intercom that there was an emergency at the other end of the hospital. Taking no further notice of the boys, the nurse turned her attention to the announcement and quickly left the counter to attend to the emergency.

"Okay, let's go, quick, before she comes back!" Ramón whispered loudly.

"Which way?"

"The second floor, that's where Grandpa was, remember?"

Miguel didn't question his cousin. He followed him faithfully to the second floor and they walked along the long empty corridor looking for their grandmother's room. At the end of the hallway Ramón saw a silhouette of a small-framed woman that looked familiar. He stood closer to the entrance of the room and looked inside. His grandmother was alone in her bed, sleeping quietly.

"Come on, Miguel, let's go tell Abuelita where we're going."

Miguel looked at his dear grandmother lying still in her oversized hospital bed and hoped that she would be able to hear what they had to tell her.

"She looks so small," Miguel said, looking down at his grandmother enshrouded by the white sheets.

"Abuelita, can you hear me?" asked Ramón. He glanced around the bed and noticed the machines that were monitoring her. Faint beeping sounds could be heard along with the soft breath of the sleeping woman.

"Does she look really sick?" Miguel asked, feeling more worried. "Maybe we shouldn't leave her. What if she dies?"

"Don't say that. She's not going to die!" Ramón said in a loud hush. "If she were super sick, the doctors would be in here doing something."

Miguel wanted to believe his cousin but he remembered what his family had said to him when their grandfather was sick in the hospital. They had reassured him that Grandpa Esteban was going to be "just fine" and "would be home soon." That was the time his grandfather had died, and now looking at his grandmother lying helpless in the mechanical bed all the painful memories of losing him rushed back.

"Abuelita, if you can hear me, squeeze my hand," Ramón said, taking the small hand in his own. "Just squeeze a little if you can."

"Can you feel anything?" Miguel asked anxiously.

"Not yet, but I know she can hear us. We have to keep trying."

From down the hall footsteps could be heard. The quick pace of the shoes walking along the linoleum floors signaled that someone was coming their way.

"Someone's coming, get behind the screen!" motioned Ramón.

Miguel moved clumsily around the bed and snuck behind a large canvas screen opposite the doorway of the room. From behind the screen, the footsteps were heard entering the room, then two voices began to speak. Ramón held his finger over his closed mouth directing his cousin to stay quiet.

"She came in yesterday and the doctor is watching her for any other reactions to the medications," the voice said matter-of-factly.

"Is she in stable condition?"

"Oh, yes, she wouldn't be on this floor if she was in any real trouble," the nurse advised. "But we need to keep her on our rotation every night for the next two weeks, the doctor was very clear."

"Has her family been contacted?"

"We've tried to call the contact person on her charts but we don't get an answer. It seems that her son is on vacation, but we'll wait for a call back."

After the room had been cleared, Ramón whispered to his cousin, "Did you hear that?"

"Yeah, she's going to be okay."

"Yeah, but not for two more weeks."

"I heard that too. Maybe she'll come home sooner," Miguel said hopefully. "Maybe we could ask the doctor."

"Are you crazy? That first lady was going to kick us out downstairs. No doctor will talk to us. We're just kids."

"You're right, we're just kids," Miguel repeated.

Ramón looked around the screen for any other unexpected visitors. Seeing none, he took his place by his grandmother's bedside and began to tell her about their plans.

"Abuelita, Miguel and I are going to be gone for a few days. We have to go find Tío Rodrigo." Ramón placed her hand into his and continued. "The doctor says you're going to be okay, you just have to rest for a while."

The boys looked at their grandmother lovingly.

"Abuelita," Miguel said, taking the other small hand into his large grip, "don't worry about us, we can take care of ourselves, you just rest for now."

Abuelita Rosa let out a soft breath and pressed her small hands into theirs.

chapter 15

It was difficult for the boys to sleep that night. Miguel kept going over the items packed in their backpacks, wondering if they had forgotten anything important. Ramón was wide awake, thinking of the long open road ahead of them and the thrill of being independent. The night passed slowly.

"Hey, maybe we should get up?" Miguel's sleepy voice asked his cousin. The morning sun had just begun to shine through the bedroom window.

Ramón had drifted to sleep just a few hours before daylight and he responded in a drowsy voice, "I'm tired, just a few more minutes."

Miguel got out of his bed and decided to get dressed. He was going to pack another pair of jeans and two T-shirts, maybe his jacket. He laced up his shoes and walked out to the kitchen. He was always hungry and the thought of doing without large quantities of food for the next several days haunted him. He took out the *chorizo*, eggs, and salsa from the refrigerator and began to make breakfast.

Ramón could smell the *chorizo* warming up in the microwave and he decided he could get up and eat. He wandered into the kitchen and took a seat at the table.

"I like my eggs well done," he ordered, watching Miguel cooking at the stove.

"I wish we had more room to take more food," said Miguel, piling eggs and *chorizo* on a large plate.

The two boys sat at the table and ate their breakfast without much conversation. They were still tired from not sleeping well the night before and their thoughts were on the trip and on their grandmother.

"Dad never called," reflected Miguel, looking down at the empty plates.

Ramón heard the disappointment in his cousin's voice and tried to console him.

"He probably got our message and is going to call the hospital first. Remember he said he didn't want to talk to us? So when he finds out that grandma's okay, he'll think he doesn't have to call us."

Miguel hung his head further. He wondered why his father wouldn't want to talk with him.

After a long silence, Ramón said thoughtfully, "This trip is going to be huge, you know? I mean, it's going to be something."

"Yeah, I know," Miguel replied, looking out of the kitchen window toward the road, "we have to believe that we can do it."

"We can't stay here; it's time for us to go," Ramón said. "I know we can make it to Santa Fe."

The backpacks were checked and rechecked for all the necessary inventory items. Miguel took the perishable food from the refrigerator and packed it last.

Ramón rummaged through the kitchen cabinets looking for spare change or any helpful gadgets. He pulled out the last drawer nearest to the stove and found something miraculous.

"Hey, look at this!" he shouted.

Miguel came rushing into the kitchen eager to see what his cousin had found.

"It's cash!" Ramón exclaimed.

"How much?"

Ramón unfolded the crumbling yellow envelope and took the bills out. He counted ten twenty-dollar bills, and five tens. "Looks like $250! We've got it made."

Miguel jumped around his cousin to get a better look. "Really? Let me see."

"Here, put this with the rest of the money. Looks like at least our gas is paid for," Ramón said, handing the money to Miguel.

He took the small fortune and stashed it in his jeans' front pocket.

Miguel and Ramón were ready to leave. The boys picked up the solitary sleeping bag and the two backpacks and opened the door. They took one last look behind them and closed the door.

chapter 16

"I'll tie my backpack to the front of the scooter and you'll have to wear yours on your back, the sleeping bag can go behind you," Ramón coolly ordered, pacing around the scooter parked on the driveway.

Miguel took a piece of rope and tied down the sleeping bag to the small rear luggage rack and swung the backpack over his shoulders, "Should we get gas first? Don't forget we need a map."

"Yeah, we'll go to the gas station down the road." Ramón tied his backpack to the front of the scooter, attaching it below the headlight in front of the handles.

It was still early morning when the boys drove into the dusty gas station. The attendant was unlocking the door to the convenience store and turned when he heard the hum of the scooter's engine.

The boys parked the scooter near a gas pump and Ramón was first to speak to the attendant. "Hey, do you have road maps to New Mexico?"

The attendant remembered the boys from the day before. The last time he had seen Ramón, he had been pushing the lifeless scooter down the road. He looked at it with curiosity. "Are you two driving that thing through two states?"

Ramón took offense to the attendant's condescending tone. "Yeah, she runs pretty good. We need gas, though."

The attendant raised his eyebrows at the younger boy's reply. He swung the heavy door open and walked behind the counter. Reaching behind a canister of beef jerky, he took out a folded road map. "Here you go. How much gas you need?"

"Just a few gallons for now," Ramón said, acting confident. He paid the attendant with a crisp new twenty dollar bill and picked up the road map from the counter.

The attendant put the money in the cash register and sat down on his stool in preparation for a long, inactive day. He picked up a magazine and looked from the side of the open glossy cover as the boys were walking out.

"Hey, be careful out there," he cautioned mildly.

Ramón turned to look back and nodded his head, "We'll be all right."

Miguel and Ramón acted like they knew exactly what they were doing. They filled the tank and boarded Natalie.

chapter 17

Ramón soon found out that Natalie was quick on the road despite her age. He navigated onto the highway and with a slight turn of his wrist on the hand clutch they were traveling at a good pace. He estimated the motor scooter's speed to be at least forty miles per hour. Most of the cars on the road were careful not to pass the Vespa too close. The drivers would veer to the left and a few would cross over to the other lane completely. So far, Miguel and Ramón didn't feel afraid of sharing the road with the larger vehicles.

The boys had fond memories of driving through the desert with their grandfather. His old truck had a manual transmission that only worked up to third gear, but their grandfather could get it going sixty miles per hour on the country roads. The boys would laugh as their small bodies bounced on the torn, vinyl bench seat when the old truck would hit a pothole or when their grandfather jammed the clutch. Ramón remembered the old truck as he navigated the scooter along the highway and wished his grandpa were still alive.

The interstate highway wasn't far from their grandmother's house. Within less than an hour they were on the busy four-lane highway, traveling toward their destination. Miguel was trying to keep his balance in the back of the small seat. He hadn't let go of the luggage rack since they left the gas station. The fall the day before on the driveway had scared him. He only moved his hand away from the rack to adjust his baseball cap closer to his head when the wind threatened to blow it away.

Ramón quickly learned to operate the hand gears of the scooter. He had been driving since he was twelve years old, and understood the mechanics of various vehicles.

Rodrigo had begun to teach the boys how to drive on one of his company trucks two years before. He wanted them to be independent and he thought that learning to drive a truck would help them become real men. He would take the boys to an empty shopping-center parking lot and let them take turns driving the large truck. Miguel always pushed on the accelerator too hard and could never move his foot fast enough to find the brake. Rodrigo would get mad and yell at him to stop the truck and let Ramón drive.

"Driving in the empty parking lot was an accomplishment," Ramón thought to himself while driving the Vespa. But he knew this was different. The road wasn't vacant.

Ramón pulled over to the side, took his sunglasses from his T-shirt pocket and put them on. The sun was getting brighter and he was tired of squinting his eyes. They were heading east on the freeway and the morning sun was directly in front of them.

"We should be able to make it to Flagstaff today, pretty cool, huh?" Ramón looked at Miguel who had been gazing at the side of the road into the distance and thinking of their last trip to Flagstaff. They had passed through the town a long time ago on their way to a fishing lodge with their grandfather before he died. Grandpa Esteban loved to go camping and fishing and began to take his grandsons with him when they were barely old enough to walk. He felt that the experience of being in nature was important for young men. They would sit around the campfire and their grandfather would tell stories of when he was a boy, about all the adventures he'd had growing up in the desert.

"That'll be cool," he answered Ramón as they started to drive off. "Maybe we can camp there."

Ramón also remembered their last trip with Grandpa Esteban. One night, when they were safe in their sleeping bags by the campfire, their grandfather had told them a story about Enrique, Ramón's father. Grandpa Esteban had chuckled when he told the story. He had told the boys that Enrique had a restless spirit and had always yearned for adventure even as a small boy. When he was twelve, he had taken his father's truck without permission and decided to drive to Sedona to see the famous red rocks of the desert. He snuck out of the house in the middle of the night and rolled the truck down the driveway so that no one would hear him. He drove away undetected but he hadn't planned for the gas that he would need to get there. The truck ran out of gas halfway down the interstate and a sympathetic truck driver stopped to help the stranded boy. The truck driver watched over him until Grandpa Esteban arrived. Grandpa wasn't mad when he picked up his son. On the way home, they talked about life and Enrique's plans for the future. Ramón also remembered his grandfather saying that Enrique eventually traveled to Sedona many times when he got older, that being among the red rocks made him feel happy.

Ramón's eyes felt the pressure of tears. He stopped himself from thinking any more about his dad. He missed him too much.

Miguel had started thinking about lunch. He had eaten a lot of food at breakfast but thoughts of the next meal began to occupy his mind.

Natalie smoothly hummed down the Arizona interstate carrying the boys closer to their destination, each one traveling on his own road.

chapter 18

The boys had been on the interstate almost two hours when Miguel told Ramón to pull over. Ramón scowled at his cousin's request. He wanted to stay on the road and make good time to Flagstaff but he took his cousin's feelings into consideration and pulled over to the shoulder. Miguel slowly dismounted and walked around the dirt on the side of the highway.

"I needed to stretch my legs, and I gotta go, too," he said, turning to find a tree or shrub nearby.

Ramón waited by the scooter and checked his watch. It wasn't yet noon. They could still reach Flagstaff if they didn't stop. He wanted to avoid driving at night. He knew that drivers of cars and trucks wouldn't be able to see the scooter. Miguel walked back toward Ramón, stretching his arms up over his head, and yawned big.

"Can I drive?" Miguel boldly asked.

Ramón looked at Miguel with a look of wonder. "Are you kidding, man?" He could see that Miguel really wanted to drive and so he continued, "Have you driven a motorcycle before?"

"Nat's not a motorcycle. I can drive."

Ramón didn't want to fight with his cousin, so he slowly explained the hand gears to Miguel and instructed him to stay to the far, far right of the lane. Placing his hands on the handles of the scooter he demonstrated to Miguel, "She turns real easy, like a bike, you know? You have to keep her steady."

"I know. I'm not stupid. Let me drive," Miguel said eagerly.

Ramón nervously moved aside and Miguel swung his leg over the front of the seat. Ramón then took his place on the back of the scooter.

"Start off slow or she will lurch forward," Ramón cautioned again.

"Yeah, yeah, here we go!" Miguel took control of the scooter and headed back onto the road. Ramón held on to the luggage rack and looked ahead and in back of them for passing trucks. The smaller cars seemed to be more cautious than the larger ones, they always steered away from the scooter, but the larger cars and trucks drove closer and faster. Ramón then heard the sound of a very large truck heading up quickly from behind. It was an eighteen-wheeler driving fast on their side of the road and he was not moving to the left of the lane to pass them at a safe distance.

"Miguel, move over, he's coming up quick!" Ramón shouted, wishing that he had never allowed his cousin to drive.

"What? Where? What do I do?" Miguel shouted back, turning the wrong hand gear and increasing the speed of the scooter.

"Slow down and move over, off the road!" Ramón screamed.

Miguel steered the scooter too quickly to the right and he lost control. Both boys, the two backpacks, the sleeping bag, and Natalie went flying in separate directions onto the dirt as the eighteen-wheeler roared past.

Miguel, too stunned to speak, sat motionless on the ground. Ramón stood up and felt a dull pain in his left arm. He felt his elbow and the muscle around his tricep for injuries. Nothing was broken, but he was in pain.

"You okay?" he asked Miguel.

"Yeah, that maniac almost hit us. Didn't he see us on the road?" Miguel said, trying to deflect the blame onto the other driver.

"We have to watch out for ourselves. No one is going to protect us. This scooter is too small. We shouldn't even be on this highway!" Ramón lamented, still touching his left arm.

Miguel saw that his cousin was hurt and he lowered his head. He felt bad for crashing the scooter.

"Is the scooter okay? Is it broken?"

Ramón walked over to Natalie. She was lying on her side and still running despite the bad fall. He grabbed the handles and straightened her up. "Yeah, she looks okay."

The pain in his left arm increased as he lifted the scooter.

"I don't know if I can drive right now, my arm hurts pretty bad," he admitted.

Miguel was scared to navigate the scooter again. He knew that another bad fall could wreck the scooter and that if a truck did hit them they could end up dead.

"I'll try. I'll be extra careful," he promised quickly, gathering the backpacks. He retied the sleeping bag with rope and motioned for his cousin to climb aboard, "Come on, we have to get to Flagstaff today, right?"

Ramón nodded and sat behind Miguel. They weren't going to give up now. Ramón held onto the luggage rack with his right arm and thought to himself, "It's not easy being independent, you have to be able to pick yourself up when you fall down."

chapter 19

The afternoon sun felt hot on their bare arms and faces. Miguel focused his eyes on the road and kept his speed lower so he could control the scooter. Ramón sat in the back quietly looking out at the desert on both sides of the highway.

"When you see the next truck stop, we should stop to eat and take a break," Ramón suggested from behind.

Miguel had been feeling hungry for hours and was glad to hear his cousin suggest a lunch break. He thought happily about the food packed in the backpacks and thought he would eat a chocolate bar first when they stopped. In the distance, he saw signs that indicated that there was a gas station and diner up ahead. He slowed down and took the exit indicated by the road sign. The exit road curved away from the highway and led up to the gas station first.

"Do we need gas?" Miguel asked, entering the station slowly.

"We'll get gas after we eat," Ramón replied.

Miguel turned the scooter around and parked in front of the small restaurant.

"Are we going to eat inside? I thought we were going to eat what we brought." Miguel said.

Ramón was first to get off of the scooter. "We should go inside and order a Coke and check the map. Then we can eat our own food."

Miguel was glad to go inside the diner. He thought it would be nice to sit in a comfortable booth away from the sun for a while. The two boys took their backpacks off the scooter and headed inside the restaurant. They chose a booth close to the door and slid onto the bench seats. The waitress came over and asked the boys what they wanted. They each ordered a large Coke. Ramón took out the map and opened it up on the table.

"This is where we are," he said, pointing to a tiny spot on the map.

"How far is Flagstaff?" asked Miguel, finishing his Coke quickly. The crushed ice sat at the bottom of the cup and he slurped the rest of the brown fizzy liquid with a straw.

"Looks like another hundred miles or so," winced Ramón. He didn't like thinking about sitting on the back of the scooter for the rest of the day.

The door to the diner swung open and a man with two young boys entered. They walked over to the empty booth next to Miguel and Ramón and sat down. Ramón could tell from their conversation that it was a father with his sons. They were talking about heading to Flagstaff too. Ramón's ears listened closely to their plans.

"But, Dad, you promised we could stop at the Grand Canyon this time. Why can't we?" pleaded the smaller boy.

"I have to get this load to Albuquerque by tomorrow or we don't get paid. We don't have time to stop." The dad waived his hand to the waitress to bring him a menu. "Besides, we can stop on the way back, when we're not in a rush."

His sons stared at the menus and ordered mechanically when the waitress returned. Miguel overheard the boys ordering cheeseburgers and fries, and his stomach began to growl.

"Ramón, can't we just eat here? We have some money," Miguel implored, not realizing that he was speaking loud enough for the other table to hear.

"We better not. We have to save what money we have in case of an emergency," Ramón answered, folding the map. "Let's go, we'll eat outside."

The father in the next booth heard the conversation. He knew what it was like to be on the road without money and hungry for food. "Boys, why don't you join us for lunch. My treat," he said, rising up from the bench and telling his sons to scoot over to make room.

Miguel's eyes opened wider and he looked at Ramón for his consent to join the other table. Ramón was really hungry too and the thought of eating a cheeseburger sounded great.

"Are you sure?" Ramón asked the man shyly.

"Yeah, come on over. These are my sons, Coy and Roy, and I'm Jake."

Jake was tall and thin. He wore a a stained trucker's cap and a plaid shirt over a dull gray T-shirt. His sons were dressed in similar clothing. "Waitress, could we have two more orders of burgers and fries, please?"

Miguel and Ramón took their places in the booth, sharing the same side of the bench seat. The plates of food arrived quickly and the observant waitress filled Miguel's glass with more Coke.

"So, where are you two headed?" Jake asked.

Seeing that Miguel's mouth was stuffed full of fries, Ramón answered. "We're going to meet up with our family."

Jake looked at Ramón, then glanced at Miguel. He tried to figure out how old they were. Miguel was tall but had a young face. Ramón was an average size for a boy of fourteen but had an experienced way about him. Jake looked back at Miguel and asked him the question the cousins wanted to avoid.

"Miguel, you're older right?"

"Oh, yeah, I'm driving my cousin around, you know, until he can get his license," Miguel answered quickly. He sat up straight and tried to look sixteen in front of the strangers.

Ramón sensed his cousin's anxiety and added, "Yeah, our parents are meeting us in Flagstaff."

Jake nodded his head and continued to chew his french fries.

"It's a good time of year to be on the road. I remember driving down the interstate into New Mexico one winter. Man, was it cold. It snows out there, you know, and these rigs slide real easy on the icy roads." He paused and took another bite of the roast beef sandwich. "What are you driving?"

"A Vespa. It's been running pretty good," said Ramón.

The man smiled and looked outside the window at the blue scooter parked outside. He remembered when he was fifteen years old and drove a dirt bike through the desert to visit his first girlfriend. The memories carried him away while the four boys finished their lunch.

"Have you guys ever been to the Grand Canyon?" Coy, the smaller boy, asked.

"We were supposed to go with our grandfather before he got sick," answered Miguel. His stomach finally felt full but he asked the waitress for another order of fries. "Hey, Ramón, maybe we should stop there on our way. I mean, if we have time."

Ramón had always wanted to see the Grand Canyon. He remembered that their grandfather had described it as one of the great wonders of the world and told them how lucky they were to live close by. "It's crazy that people can live so near one of the world's greatest treasures and never make the effort to spend time there," Grandpa Esteban had said. So Ramón answered Miguel, "Coy and Roy have to see it. They need to see how amazing the world can be."

Grandpa Esteban had gone into the hospital before they could take the trip to the canyon and Rodrigo had promised for the last two years to take Miguel and Ramón but could never schedule the time away from his business.

"You should go on your scooter!" Coy said with boyish enthusiasm.

"Yeah, Ramón," Miguel added. "Lets go while we have the chance!" Miguel was forgetting that his cousin had told Jake that they were heading to Flagstaff.

"You just stay on the interstate. The road signs will point the way," Jake said, placing money on the table for the waitress. "Sometimes you have to take the road that opens up before you, even if you haven't planned on going in that particular direction."

Jake winked at the two cousins and smiled a knowing smile, then added, "You're only young once. When you get older, adventures don't come around that much."

Ramón considered the thoughtful words of the man. As they left the diner, he thought to himself, "Yeah, we'll go if the signs point the way."

chapter 20

Miguel was getting better at driving the scooter. He was careful to turn the gears on the handle slowly and he watched for traffic with a keener eye. Ramón sat behind him. His arm was still sore but he soon forgot about the pain. They were entering a national forest that was filled with aspen trees. As Ramón looked into the immense grove, he saw thousands of tall trees standing side by side with their textured white bark and bright green leaves glistening in the afternoon sunlight. They were clustered close together and the picture they made was beautiful. Ramón thought that it would be great to get lost wandering around the trees.

When Ramón was younger he painted. Often, after the camping trips with their grandfather, he would draw and paint the impressions that were left with him from the trip. Sometimes the pictures included people, others just the mountains and the sky. His grandmother would say that he could see things that other people couldn't, that he saw things differently. An art teacher had once commented that Ramón had an "artist's eye." Painting made Ramón happy. But he had stopped painting after his grandfather died. Nothing looked the same to Ramón after Grandpa Esteban was gone.

As the road and the forest passed by, he felt further and further away from home. Everything felt new. It felt like his past was behind him. Ramón envisioned the tall trees on a painter's canvas. Shades of white and green appeared in his mind. The vision of the tall aspens had awakened his sleeping imagination.

Miguel noticed the sign for the Grand Canyon first. "Hey, Ramón," he shouted back to his cousin, "did you see the sign? Let's go."

Ramón was lost in his own thoughts, still gazing at the tall trees. He took a moment then replied, "Yeah, we should stop soon and find a place to camp."

Miguel took the road leading to the Grand Canyon National Park. The entrance to the park was unattended and they drove through unnoticed. Miguel followed the road signs directing traffic to the southern rim of the canyon. Driving around the connecting roads, he looked for a place to park and for a safe place to sleep. He noticed that many of the tourists had trailers to sleep in, while an adventurous few camped outside in tents.

Seeing a public rest stop in a secluded area, he decided to pull in. Both boys were glad to stop for the night. The first day was exhausting and Ramón's arm was starting to hurt again.

As Miguel untied the sleeping bag from the front of the scooter, he felt something hit his foot. He looked down and saw a soccer ball rolling on the ground.

"Hey, sorry about that," the voice said.

Miguel looked around and saw a boy his age running toward him.

"Jason can't kick a ball straight. I'm surprised he hasn't kicked it into the canyon yet," the boy said, laughing. He picked up the soccer ball and looked at the two boys and Natalie leaning on her metal stand. "Hey, are you guys driving that around?"

Miguel stood up straight and was eager to impress the stranger. "Yeah, we're on a road trip to New Mexico, been driving all day."

"No way!" the boy said with surprise, and added, "by yourselves?"

Ramón jumped into the conversation.

"Yeah, it goes pretty fast, we're driving with the big rigs on the highway. Miguel crashed, though. We got pretty banged up," he bragged.

The stranger was impressed. He turned to Miguel and said, "We're camping out along the rim over there." He pointed behind him. "I'll ask our adviser if you can join us."

Before Miguel or Ramón could reply, the boy ran off with the soccer ball across the parking lot. He returned with a young man who looked about twenty years old.

"This is Turner, he's our adviser for the trip. I'm Chris," the new boy said. Turner was actually in his late twenties but looked young for his age. He smiled at the boys and shook their hands.

"How are you guys doing?" Turner asked, looking at the scooter from the corner of his eye.

"I'm Miguel and this is Ramón, my cousin."

"Are you guys all alone out here?"

"We're on our way to New Mexico. We're doing all right," Ramón said, swinging his backpack on his good arm.

Turner had been working with youth groups since he had been old enough to be an adviser on his first camping trip. He was a good mentor and understood that young men needed guidance through life. He also could accurately detect the ages of the two boys standing in front of him and was perplexed by their travel plans.

"So, who's older?" Turner asked, not wanting to reveal the true nature of his question.

"I am," Miguel replied. He had become more comfortable with his new identity on the road and could answer the question without hesitation.

"So, you're in high school?" Turner continued.

"Oh, yeah, I've just got two more years to go," Miguel answered, hoping he had calculated correctly.

Turner smiled at the boys and decided he would make further inquiries later. He could see that the boys were tired and hungry.

"Why don't you join us for dinner, and if you don't have anywhere to sleep, you can camp out with us. We're sleeping out in the open tonight by campfire," Turner said.

Turner had seen their one sleeping bag, which was now lying on the asphalt, and figured that the boys were not well-equipped to handle a night alone in the desert.

Miguel was hungry again and the idea of sleeping around a campfire sounded fun, "What do you think, Ramón?" he asked, looking at his cousin.

Ramón adjusted the backpack on his right shoulder and agreed to the generous offer.

chapter 21

The boys wheeled the scooter and their belongings to the campsite and met the other boys. The soccer ball was being kicked around on a grassy area nearby and Turner was getting the food out of several ice chests. Miguel saw the boys playing soccer and wanted to join in. His legs were stiff from sitting on the small seat all day and he wanted to run around and stretch out. He approached the game in progress and when the ball rolled in his direction, he kicked it up with the end of his shoe and balanced it on his knee before kicking it up and forward to the other players.

"Hey, he's good. You're with us," Chris said, running toward Miguel to take the pass. "You play on a team?"

"Yeah, next year I'll play varsity." Miguel spoke with reservation in his voice. After the last fight at school, the principal had wanted to expel Miguel and his dad had threatened that he would never let him play soccer again if he didn't "straighten up."

Not being able to play soccer was Miguel's biggest fear. He had started to play when he was four years old and was the most outstanding player on every team he played on. He was taller than most boys his age and his muscles were more developed than his teammates' but that did not affect his speed on the field. The other kids back home used to call him "Tank" because when he had control of the ball no one could stop him. The school coach had been impressed with Miguel and for the last two years had encouraged him to train harder and focus on his natural athletic ability. Deep in his heart, Miguel wanted to play soccer forever. Even if he never played professionally, he knew that playing soccer was his special gift and that he would only be happy if he could play. Now at fourteen, his future was at risk due to his bad grades and his recent bad behavior.

The boys played for a long time until the inevitable darkness stopped them. Turner had cooked chili dogs over the campfire and was passing around bags of potato chips and plates full of spicy food when the boys returned from the game. Ramón was stretched out by the fire, eating his second chili dog when Miguel saw him.

"These are awesome," Ramón said with his mouth full. "Who won?"

"Miguel beat us all," Chris said, laughing. "I've never seen anyone like him, and I play in tournaments all the time!"

Ramón knew that his cousin was a great soccer player. He admired his ability and frequently attended his soccer games, especially the championship tournaments. Ramón nodded at Chris's observation and motioned for Miguel to sit nearby.

"Turner says you guys are driving to New Mexico on your own. Is that true?" asked another boy.

"Santa Fe, actually," Miguel said proudly, feeling the admiration from the group after his dominance on the newly created soccer field. "My mom and dad left two days ago, and we're meeting them there." Miguel didn't mention that they had been left behind and that his father had no idea that they were on the road by themselves.

The boys were in awe. For the rest of the night, Miguel or Ramón could have told them the most fantastic stories and their newfound friends would have believed every word. But Miguel and Ramón were honest about themselves and soon the conversation drifted to what their school was like and the different activities they were involved in. Turner asked about the classes they were taking and if they liked school. Ramón tried to act like everything was okay but soon he felt like he had to get everything off his chest.

"Miguel and I almost got kicked out of school last month," he blurted out while Turner passed around chocolate chip cookies from a box.

"What happened?" Turner asked. "It must have been serious for the school to want to expel you."

Ramón took a cookie and bit into it. "Miguel was fighting this kid. He was winning at first but then two other guys jumped in and started punching Miguel. That's three against one and I couldn't just stand there. I had to get into the mix!"

The others listened and their admiration grew even more. Miguel and Ramón were real heroes in their eyes, tough guys who could make it on their own and fight back if they had to. Chris spoke first.

"Why were you fighting in the first place? I mean, what started it?"

Ramón looked to Miguel to tell the story.

"Well, there was this guy, not really a friend of mine but I knew him from grade school. We played on the same soccer team when we were kids," he stopped and took the last bite of his third chili dog. "He's kinda small, he didn't grow much after fifth grade, and this other guy was pushing him around and it looked like he was going to get real hurt. He was throwing him up against a brick wall."

Ramón stayed silent as Miguel continued.

"I got in the middle of it and pushed the other guy on the ground, when he got up his other friends jumped in and it got rough. That's when Ramón tried to help."

"Did you explain that to the principal, did you tell him why you got involved in that fight?" Turner asked with a concerned tone in his voice.

"Yeah, we both did," said Miguel, looking at his cousin. "But I guess that other guy's dad, the one I beat up, is on the school board or something. He didn't get in trouble. We did."

"What about your parents, what did they say?" Turner asked.

"My dad was real mad after the principal told him that the fight was my fault. He wouldn't listen when I tried to tell him what really happened. Then it only got worse when I got in trouble the second time," Miguel explained.

Everyone was listening with rapt attention.

"A couple of days later, the guy I beat up jumped me after school in the parking lot, with his older brother. I'm bigger than the both of them, though, so I didn't get hurt, but his older brother ended up with a broken nose, I think." Miguel smiled a little when he remembered the older brother crying on the ground with blood coming out of his nose.

"He had to defend himself, those guys were trying to mess him up. What was he supposed to do?" Ramón asked, feeling his emotions rise as his cousin retold the story. "I even got blamed for the second fight and I wasn't even there!"

Turner sat down and faced Miguel. "You did what you had to do, you had no choice. Those boys attacked your friend and could have really hurt him. It was good that you interceded. You did the right thing."

"I wish my dad thought so," Miguel said, mournfully remembering the lost cell phones and video games.

"Keep telling him the truth. One day he'll hear you," consoled Turner. "Your dad just wants you to have a good future. He's worried that if you get into trouble at school, it will affect the rest of your life."

"I remember when my little brother was getting picked on by a bully last year and we had to change schools because my parents couldn't stop it. Maybe I should have beat him up," interjected a red-haired boy almost the same size as Miguel. "I could have taken him."

"If you get the first punch in you have a better chance at winning the fight!" Ramón suggested eagerly.

"Beating someone up isn't always the answer," Turner quickly stated. "Sometimes, only sometimes, violence is appropriate. I do think Miguel did the right thing. Don't worry about your dad, Miguel. I'm sure he'll understand someday."

Miguel ate the stack of cookies in his hand, stared into the firelight, and thought to himself, "Why can't my dad understand me *now*?"

chapter 22

The campfire kept all the boys warm as they slept through the night. Ramón had opened up the sleeping bag to the size of one flat blanket and he and his cousin slept on it next to the open flames.

Since Ramón had been a little boy, he had often dreamed of his father. If he was upset or sad, his dad would appear in a dream and talk to him. But as he got older, Ramón rarely dreamed of Enrique. Ramón began to feel increasingly alone. Not having a dad around was hard for a young boy and now that he was becoming a man, he had no one to guide him through life. Rodrigo was a good uncle but it wasn't the same thing. Rodrigo was Miguel's dad, not his, and Ramón felt the difference in the ways he heard Rodrigo speak to Miguel. Ramón wanted his dad back. He needed him.

Warmed by the fire, in a deep comfortable sleep, Ramón began to dream. It was the same dream he had dreamed as a child. Enrique was driving the family car, talking to him in the back seat. Ramón never saw his dad's face, he could only see the back of his head, but he knew it was him. During the first part of the dream, Ramón felt safe with his dad driving and he felt himself laugh when his dad teased him with a joke. Then the car suddenly swerved and the dream went dark. Ramón woke up suddenly and found himself at the campsite.

"Hey, man, you okay?" Miguel asked with one eye still closed. "You were shouting something."

Ramón sat still and tried to keep the vision of his dad in his head for as long as he could. For a few more minutes he could feel like his dad was still alive.

The sun was just beginning to rise and a few of the other boys had woken up. Turner was rummaging through the group's van looking for more camping gear and turned when he heard Ramón walking toward him.

"Did you sleep okay?" Turner asked.

"Yeah, I'm all right." Ramón was now feeling the emptiness of being alone in the world.

"After breakfast, we're going to head out on a short hike down into the canyon. Why don't you join us?"

Ramón wasn't sure how he felt about anything at that moment. Everything seemed impossible and the road to Santa Fe seemed long and endless.

"I don't know. I'll ask Miguel," he answered quietly.

Miguel was exhausted from the drive the day before and only the inviting smell of the frying sausages woke him up from his slumber. He had dreamed of playing at a World Cup soccer game and as usual he scored the winning goal. He got up from the sleeping bag, took a plate of sausages nestled over chili beans, and started to eat.

"What do you think of going on a hike into the canyon with the others?" Ramón asked his cousin.

"Yeah, that sounds cool if we can spare the time."

Ramón then remembered his grandfather's wishes of taking them to the canyon and replied, "Yeah, we're okay on time. Let's do it." Ramón took a few small bites of sausage and breathed in the fresh morning air. "Today is a new day," he thought, "we'll see what happens."

chapter 23

When the campsite was cleared, Turner split the boys into smaller groups. Three teams of five were organized for the hike down the canyon. Each team would watch for their own members and he would trail behind the three teams to make sure that no one got left behind. This was his fifth trip to the canyon and he knew every turn of the hiking trail.

"Okay, boys, let's go. Chris, you're taking your team down first," Turner said, motioning for Chris to start the hike.

Miguel and Ramón were on Chris's team and began to walk toward the trail with the other boys.

The southern rim of the canyon was crowded with trees, shrubs, and rocks. The stunning views of the Grand Canyon could only be seen from certain vantage points. Even though they had been sleeping on the edge of the great wonder, the boys had not yet seen the surprising sight. Miguel followed Chris toward the entrance to the trail and when they reached an open clearing he saw the canyon for the first time. He advanced slowly and turned his head in all directions in disbelief of its size.

"No way! This thing is huge! Hey, Ramón, you gotta see this!" he exclaimed.

Ramón reached his cousin's side and looked out into the great expanse. The walls of rock that lined the canyon were layered with shades of pink, brown, beige, and gray. The curves in the wide canyon walls undulated like ocean currents and the depth of the opening felt incomprehensible. Ramón had never seen anything like it before. He stood, turning his head to the right, then to the left, trying to take in the full view.

"This is crazy." He said to himself. "How did it get here?"

Chris, who had been on the same trip to the canyon last year, spoke up when he heard Ramón's question. "It took millions of years to form. Look at the various layers of rock, at all the different colors. Each one is a different stage of time. Pretty cool, huh?"

They started down the trail one by one, proceeding carefully but trying to keep their eyes on the majesty of the earth around them. After descending down the trail a quarter of a mile, Turner stopped the boys and they took a break off to the side at a point designated for sightseeing. Ramón sat facing the canyon and continued to gaze in wonder at what he saw. The morning sun was illuminating one side of the canyon while the other side was in shadows. The colors of the rock were varied depending on the light and the shadows being cast upon them. Ramón wished he had his sketch book with him to capture the images. Off to the side, he saw a tourist taking pictures of the canyon, while others posed with their friends in a huddle blocking the canyon's view.

"Someday," he thought, "I'll paint this, just how it looks now."

"So what do you think?" Turner asked Ramón.

"It's pretty cool."

"This canyon is more than just a natural wonder. It represents the mystery and capacity each person has inside of them to do great things."

Ramón kept his eyes on the magnificent view.

"Do you think everyone can be great?"

"We all originated from the same awesome source, and each one of us has their own unique talents. Once we discover what that talent is, we can be as great as we allow ourselves to be."

Turner didn't rush the boys through the hike. He allowed them to walk slowly and to admire the open space surrounding them. He checked on all the groups, then approached Miguel and Ramón at the end of the trail.

"So, boys, I guess you're heading to New Mexico later?"

"Yeah," Miguel answered. He sat back on a large rock and let the morning sun warm his face. "We have a lot more road to cover."

Turner smiled at the young boy's confidence and turned to Ramón. "Sometimes life gives us opportunities to prove to ourselves how great we can actually be, and sometimes we have to trust that we can achieve the impossible."

Miguel overheard Turner's words to his cousin and added, "Yeah, my dad always says that only real men attempt the impossible."

Ramón thought about Turner's words and wondered about himself and his future, then he turned and said, "I think we have to get back on the road." He had remembered the purpose of the trip and was suddenly eager to get back on the road.

"I'm glad you came along," said Turner. "We take this trip every year at the beginning of the summer. Here's our club information if you want to join us in the future." Turner handed Ramón a flyer with a list of phone numbers and e-mail addresses.

"Next summer we're conducting a tour of the bottom of the canyon and we might even go river rafting. You could bring your dad."

Miguel's heart skipped a beat when he thought of his dad joining them on a river rafting adventure, and he could not contain his excitement. "That would be awesome!"

"Yeah, maybe we will. Thanks a lot for everything," Ramón said, adjusting his backpack. "Let's go, Miguel."

"You have my phone number on that paper. If you need to call me over the next few days, go ahead," the young man offered with sincerity.

Turner shook their hands and allowed the boys to leave the safety of the group. During their stay, Turner could see that Ramón had a lack of direction and that Miguel lacked self discipline. The young counselor knew that they were on a big adventure and that they needed to continue on their journey to prove to themselves that they could do it.

Miguel and Ramón ascended the canyon wall, passing those who were making the descent.

"We'll be back, Miguel," Ramón promised, sensing that his cousin was reluctant to leave his new friends. "There's a lot more to see. This is only the beginning."

chapter 24

The town of Flagstaff breezed by as Miguel turned the hand gear of the scooter and increased his speed on the interstate. Another national forest would have to be driven through before they reached Sedona. The road began to curve slightly and Miguel slowed his speed. Once in the national forest, the road narrowed and became two lanes. The left side of the road was bordered by cliff walls made of rock and the right side descended into small valleys filled with abundant trees and a steady stream of water running through the center.

Ramón closed his eyes and allowed himself to feel the mountains as they passed. He heard the water ripple below. The spirit of the open road had captured him and he raised his arms above his head to experience the feeling of freedom. He felt liberated from his own life and everything he had known before. Ramón opened his eyes and felt a strange sense of happiness and hope.

The road sign directing traffic to Sedona indicated that the mystical town was only a few more miles away. Miguel kept his eyes wide open so he wouldn't miss it. Natalie turned smoothly around the last curve of the road and the forest opened up onto the picturesque desert landscape. Sedona was breathtaking.

Gigantic monuments of red rock stood stoically in the distance. The rock formations were both in clusters and in perfect solitude.

Ramón was dazzled. He ordered his cousin to pull over to the side of the road so that he could take a better look. Ramón stepped onto the clay-colored soil and stared into the deep blue skies overhead. It was a dream come true. The most vivid colors and definitive shapes clearly set against a perfect stark background. Sedona was magical.

Miguel took a bottle of water from his backpack and considered if he should eat the peanuts he saw in the side pocket. He took the bag and opened it, handing it to Ramón first.

"I think these peanuts are honey roasted. I like "bar" better. I guess these are okay."

Ramón took the bag and told his cousin instinctively, "I think we should stay here tonight, I can't leave here yet."

"But we have at least four more hours of daylight. We could make it to Albuquerque tonight!" Miguel responded, feeling confident in his driving skills and exaggerating the nearness of Albuquerque.

"Let's drive into the town and check it out," Ramón said, ignoring Miguel's suggestion. He wasn't ready to drive through the magical place. Something told him that he needed to be there, and he wasn't leaving.

Miguel ate the rest of the peanuts and decided to save the tempting chocolate bar for later. Ramón climbed on the scooter and they continued their drive toward the town, through the red rocks, into the magic of the desert.

chapter 25

The town plaza was filled with parked cars and people walking on the sidewalks. Restaurants and art galleries lined the main street with the majestic red rocks looming in the distance. Miguel drove up to a gas station and filled the tank. Ramón looked around and decided to explore.

"Hey, I'm going over to the main street to check it out. I'll be back in a while, or do you wanna come?" he said.

"No, it's okay. I'll take Nat to the park over there. I need to sleep," Miguel answered, staring longingly at a patch of shade trees across the street.

Ramón took a bottle of water from the side pocket of his backpack and walked in the direction of the busy town.

It was late afternoon and a warm desert breeze washed over the buildings and wandering tourists. Ramón sipped the bottled water, walking slowly down the sidewalks with the other travelers. He looked into the windows of the shops and art galleries. Window after window displayed bronze sculptures, colorful glass creations, and wood carvings. But what captured Ramón's attention were the endless collections of paintings. Scenes of the desert, wandering rivers, and the glorious red rocks depicted on canvas after canvas. Some were painted in oil, others in watercolor, but all of them captured the unique vision of individual artists. "I can do this," he thought to himself. "I feel what they see."

He found a bench across from a large gallery window and sat down with his backpack next to him. The paintings in the window were being rearranged by the shop owner. The man moved each large canvas carefully and occasionally took a step back to analyze the new display. After several attempts to rearrange the art pieces, he walked outside of the shop and stood directly in front of the window next to the bench where Ramón was sitting.

"I think you should place the larger picture off to the side, the colors of the smaller picture will look better if they are in the middle of the group," Ramón wisely suggested.

The shop owner looked around to see who had made the interesting observation and was shocked to see the young man sitting on the bench.

"Do you really think so?" the man asked.

"Yeah, try it," Ramón suggested, still staring at the window.

From behind the glass, the canvases were reorganized as Ramón had suggested. The shop owner then came out and assessed the window display with a critical eye.

"It does look better, much better," he said approvingly. "Do you live around here? Do I know your parents?"

"No, we're just passing through."

"You've got a sharp eye," the man complimented. "I appreciate the help. Come inside and I'll show you the gallery."

Ramón was surprised at the man's kind offer and accepted the invitation. He walked into the sophisticated shop, surrounded by expensive paintings and sculptures waiting to be purchased by wealthy tourists. Each canvas and hand-crafted sculpture was more beautiful than the next. Ramón had never been so close to real works of art.

The shop owner graciously walked with him around the store and introduced him to the work of local and nationally recognized artists. When the tour was complete, he handed Ramón a small stack of glossy postcards depicting many of the works of art he had just seen.

"These are yours," the shop owner said in a generous voice. "I can recognize an artist in the making when I meet one. Good luck, son."

Ramón thanked the man and placed the postcards in his backpack. The kindness of the shop owner had made him feel closer to his dream of becoming an artist someday.

Time passed quickly as he continued to gaze at the captivating art works in the shop windows, but after a while Ramón realized that Miguel was probably waiting for him at the park. He took one last look and hurried back. He found Miguel snoring loudly on a park bench with his backpack placed on his chest.

"Hey, we better find a place to camp out for the night before it gets dark," Ramón said, nudging Miguel on the arm. "Get up, man. Let's go."

Miguel made one last loud snort and sat up in surprise. "What's going on? Where are we?"

Feeling the exaltation of an artist inspired by a new vision, Ramón replied, "We're in heaven. We finally made it to heaven."

chapter 26

Natalie roared up the side streets, past the center of town, into the hills inhabited by the gigantic rock formations. Ramón pointed toward a cluster of red rocks in the distance for Miguel to navigate to. The sun was beginning to set below thin wisps of clouds. Ramón turned to see the pale red earth turn to brilliant orange and the blue sky filling with streaks of pink, lavender, and gray. The metamorphosis of color was perfectly orchestrated by nature. Miguel drove around the cluster of rough rock into a cavern on the western side so they could view the sunset and the town below.

There were old tree branches and dried brush lying around the rocks. Miguel gathered the twigs and brush and piled them on the ground to make a fire. He took the matches from his backpack and lit the brush, then slowly fanned the smoke into flames. Ramón took out the wrapped burritos from the backpack and decided their rations for the night. He decided that they would eat one burrito each and split one of the chocolate bars for dessert.

Miguel looked disapprovingly at the single burrito sitting on the sleeping bag. "Is that all we're eating?" he asked, taking note of the candy bar in Ramón's hand.

"We'll have one burrito tonight and one in the morning. That leaves only one more ration for tomorrow's lunch," Ramón said, unwrapping his burrito and taking a bite.

"I don't understand why we can't eat regular food. We have the extra money. Look, it's here in my pocket!" Miguel was getting upset. He remembered seeing his favorite fast food restaurant in the town just minutes before.

"That money doesn't even belong to us. It's Abuelita's, and we're not going to spend it unless we have to. It's for an emergency, remember?"

Miguel thought of his grandmother lying still in her hospital bed. The excitement of the trip had kept his thoughts away from her but now, in the quiet of the desert, he began to think of her and wondered how she was.

"Ramón, you think we did the right thing leaving Abuelita?"

"The nurses said she was going to be okay. We have to believe that," Ramón replied solemnly.

"Besides," Ramón added, "I know in my heart she's okay, don't you?"

Miguel smiled, feeling reassured by his cousin's insight, "Yeah, I do."

"I said a prayer for her last night before I fell asleep," Ramón confessed quietly.

"I did, too," Miguel answered.

They sat on the hard ground and ate their dinner. Miguel ate the burrito in three bites. Ramón gave in and allowed him to also eat one of the granola bars along with one half of the chocolate bar.

Still hungry, Miguel sat back against the rock wall and looked down at the town beginning to light up in the darkness. "It feels like we're really far away, huh?" he said.

"Yeah, I've been thinking that all day."

"Those guys at the Grand Canyon were cool. I wouldn't mind going back to the canyon next year," Miguel added.

"There's a lot we should do," pondered Ramón, "there's so much to see. I mean, look at this place, just think of how many more places like this are there in the world. We could probably travel nonstop for the rest of our lives and never see everything there is out there."

"Hey, man, we could, you know, travel our whole lives." Miguel's imagination sprung into action. "We could drop outta school and just drive Nat around. We wouldn't need a lot of money. We would work along the way. But we would need another sleeping bag, though."

Ramón laughed at Miguel's idea. "Yeah, just drive around seeing the sights and begging for food, that sounds awesome."

"No, I mean it, at least once a year or something, take a trip somewhere. See something new!"

"If Grandpa Esteban was still here, he would understand," said Ramón, closing his eyes to feel the last of the sun's rays on his face.

"I'm going to tell my dad to take us places. We need to see the world."

"Yeah, we'll tell Tío Rodrigo after he's done yelling at us. He might be real mad when we see him, you know? Did you ever think of that?"

Miguel's excitement left his face.

"My dad cares about us, I just wish . . . I just wish he could remember what it was like to be young." He took a long pause then continued, "We had to do this, we had to go on our own."

Ramón took a long wood stick lying off to the side of the fire and stuck it into the flames. "If my dad were here, he would understand."

Both boys sat in silence, leaning against the side of the enormous red rock with the soft firelight flickering in their eyes.

chapter 27

The rocky cavern provided adequate shelter for the boys. The desert winds blew from the southeast and the large expanse of stone shielded them as they slept. Miguel had stacked extra branches nearby and in accordance with their original plan, Miguel suggested that Ramón use the sleeping bag first. They found spots on the ground that were the most comfortable and used the backpacks and extra clothes as pillows.

Ramón fell asleep first. The sleeping bag was large and he nestled into it while feeling the heat of the flames on his face. Being next to the giant red rocks made him feel safe despite being out in the desert alone. He slept the first part of the night easily. Then the first of two dreams came.

He was driving the scooter along an ocean coastline. The road was extremely narrow and on the left side of the road was a steep cliff which dropped off sharply into the crashing waves below. The road was dangerous and the scooter was leaning toward the cliff, closer every minute he traveled. Ramón steered the scooter away from the cliff but no matter how far to the right he turned the handles, the scooter drifted to danger. It felt like no matter what he did to drive the scooter away from the dangerous cliff, he was going to fall onto the rocks below.

Ramón woke up for a moment and turned over in the sleeping bag. The heat of the fire warmed his back and he saw Miguel placing more wood on top of the flames. The warmth of the fire quickly put him back to sleep.

Then the second dream came. Ramón was standing on open ground. There were no buildings or people; all he could see was a flat horizon of empty desert. He looked for a road or a sign for direction but nothing was there. He was completely alone. Strong winds began to blow and in an instant all visibility was gone. He could see nothing but clouds of dust and dirt swirling around him. The sky darkened and he covered his mouth to avoid breathing in the dust. Out of the darkness appeared two beams of lights. As the lights grew stronger, he heard the roar of a familiar engine. An old truck pulled up in front of him and Grandpa Esteban stepped out.

"Hey, there, we've been looking for you," Grandpa Esteban said, taking off his cowboy hat and dusting it with his hand. "Your dad and I have been worried, we didn't think you'd be able to find us in all this dust. It's quite a storm, isn't it?"

Ramón stood speechless, looking at his beloved grandfather. The older man was still wearing his worn work boots and driving the same old pickup truck that he and Miguel used to take rides in.

Ramón wiped his eyes and refocused on the apparition. "Is it really you?" he asked in a whisper.

"It's okay, Ramón, come here and give your grandpa a hug."

Ramón ran to his grandpa and threw his arms around his barrel-sized chest. "I'm so glad you're here, I thought I was lost. I couldn't see anything, how did you find me?" he asked.

"We never lose sight of where you are or what you're doing. We've been following you all the way since you and Miguel left the house. This old truck can keep up with anything, but I need to check the brakes, they've been squeaking lately."

"We went to the Grand Canyon, Grandpa. You were right, it was amazing. Miguel told our friends there about what happened at school and they believed us!"

Grandpa Esteban stopped Ramón. "I know everything, son. I'm so proud of you and Miguel because you're on the right path. But you have a long way to go, you have to promise to be careful and think about the choices you make in life, okay?"

Ramón looked into the old man's kind eyes and nodded his head. At that moment, he saw another man step out of the passenger side of the truck. The figure was hard to see at first then he realized who it was. It was his dad.

"Ramón, this is your father, Enrique," Grandpa Esteban announced, taking a step back from his grandson.

Enrique walked slowly toward Ramón. He resembled Tío Rodrigo, but looked many years younger. Both father and son stood looking at one another in disbelief.

"I wasn't sure if I would ever have the chance to meet you as a young man," Enrique said. His voice trembled as he held out his arms, "I've never stopped loving you. Can you forgive me, *mijo*?"

"Dad? Is that really you?" Ramón looked at the familiar face and flashes of the pictures in his grandmother's house filled his mind. Enrique looked so young, like he did in the pictures. Ramón took a step toward his father and touched his hands, they were strong and warm, but he dared not look into his eyes, fearing that he wasn't real.

Ramón fell into his father's strong arms, shutting his eyes tight. Feeling all the strength of his father's embrace, he stood there in silence, trying to absorb all the affection that he had never before had the chance to feel.

"Why did you have to go? Why did you leave us?" Ramón could no longer restrain the tears and started to cry.

"It was my time, *mijo*, I had no choice."

"But I needed you, I still need you." Ramón's voice quivered as he spoke.

"I'm so sorry. We can't control when we are born or when it's time to die, I know that now."

"But what about me? What am I supposed to do?" begged Ramón.

Enrique's eyes swelled with tears and he strengthened his embrace around Ramón. "I will always watch over you, even when you think that I'm not there. Look for me in your dreams and in the stars at night. I am forever with you. You're my life."

Ramón felt the loving embrace of his father as the dust clouds stopped swirling and the sky became brighter. The truck lights faded and with the lightness of the day, the dream was over.

Miguel managed to sleep for a few hours during the night and was stirring the fire when Ramón woke up. He had heard Ramón talking in his sleep but wasn't sure what he was saying. He knew that his cousin missed his dad terribly. Miguel thought of their grandmother crying on Tío Enrique's birthday and when they would go to the cemetery. Miguel also recalled how his father would walk away from Tío Enrique's grave not wanting anyone see him cry. Ramón moved in the sleeping bag and turned toward the warm morning fire.

"It was pretty cold last night," Miguel said, putting more sticks on the fire. "You're lucky you had the sleeping bag."

Ramón stayed quiet and did not respond. He closed his eyes and tried to remember his father's face and the sound of his voice.

"Hey, guess what I saw just a minute ago?" Miguel's eyes lit up and he looked directly at his cousin, hoping he would listen.

"What, what happened?"

"As the sun was coming up, there was an eagle flying around over our rocks. It came real close and landed on the top of the rock where we were sleeping!" Miguel exclaimed, "Isn't that something? A real eagle, and he was big. I didn't know they were that big!"

"Oh, yeah?" responded Ramón, slightly interested. "Why would it come here?"

"Maybe he's here to watch over us. He had a strange look in his eyes, like he knew who we were or something."

Ramón felt a pang in his heart and he knew instantly why the eagle had been there. He closed his eyes and quietly told his father that he loved him.

chapter 28

"How many more miles to Albuquerque?" Miguel asked, looking for the map in Ramón's backpack.

"Probably three hundred or so, maybe more."

Ramón finished rolling the sleeping bag and started tying it down on the scooter.

"You gotta be kidding me. That far?"

"Yeah, we better get going."

Ramón wheeled Natalie over toward the dirt road and motioned for him to get on board. "I'll drive for a while. My arm doesn't hurt that bad."

Miguel was still tired from the night before and was glad not to have the responsibility of watching the road. He climbed onto the back of the scooter and let Ramón lead the way.

The interstate led them out of Sedona and into secluded desert country. The boys traveled for miles without seeing any buildings, or even road signs. All that was visible was the endless stretch of black asphalt road and the gray silhouettes of mountains in the distance.

Ramón drove steadily. He was glad to have the road to focus on. As the black asphalt melted underneath the wheels, blue cloudless skies hung overhead. It was a perfect desert morning.

"Hey, what's that sign say?" Miguel shouted in his cousin's ear.

Ramón focused on the green piece of metal standing alone on the side of the road and said aloud, "Hot Springs, 10 Miles."

"Hey, let's go," Miguel insisted.

The boys had been traveling for almost three hours without a break and Ramón liked the idea of swimming in hot pools of water.

"Okay, but not for too long."

The exit took them down a two-lane road between a couple of small hills and into flat ground surrounded by a rocky formation. No one was around and the boys looked in amazement at the natural pools of water.

"No way! No one is here! We have this place all to ourselves!" Miguel shouted. He ran over to the nearest pool of water and put his hand in. "Its hot, like a hot tub!"

Ramón laughed and stripped off his shirt. They jumped in and laughed at the surprising heat of the water.

"This is awesome, I can't believe this is out here," said Miguel, dunking his head under the warm bubbles.

Some of the natural springs were warmer than the others. The boys took turns jumping in and out of each pool comparing the temperatures and splashing the warm water on the rocks.

After a long soak in the hottest pool, both boys got out and stretched out under the clear blue sky. The surrounding rocks were flat and comfortable to lie on. The sun's hot rays felt soothing and soon their thoughts drifted to the simple joys of boyhood.

"This is awesome," Miguel repeated. "Life should be like this all the time."

Ramón allowed the additional heat from the smooth granite rock to warm his body. He opened his eyes for a moment and replied pensively, "Our lives will be what we make of them."

"You're getting heavy. Maybe you should get out of the sun," Miguel teased.

"Whatever, man, let's get out of here. We gotta keep moving." Ramón laughed and closed his eyes for a few minutes longer, feeling the healing energy of the open desert.

chapter 29

Alternating stripes of blue, turquoise, coral, and black were stacked in the mountains. They followed one another closely, each one more colorful than the next. White stretches of clouds drifted easily over the sky and disappeared just as quickly as they formed.

Natalie hummed onward, not giving any signs of fatigue or weariness. Miguel rode along admiring the scenery and sometimes commenting to his cousin about how they should move and live in the middle of whatever mountain range was currently in view. Ramón would laugh and pretend to agree that it was a good idea. The boys were happy. Life was in perfect order and the future seemed boundless. The road had become their source of inspiration.

They were making good progress toward the New Mexico state border when Miguel saw something that caught his eye. A group of blue tents was pitched below a cluster of mountains along with a few white trailers.

"What's going on over there?" he asked, pointing to get Ramón's attention.

Ramón looked out toward the sight and said, "Looks like some campers."

"That's a lot of tents to be just campers, let's go check it out."

"Miguel, we have to keep going."

"Maybe we should stop anyway. We don't know how much further before we see a town. We also need to find a place to sleep for the night." Miguel knew that Ramón would agree to stop if he made it sound like he was concerned for their safety.

Ramón took a dirt road which appeared to lead to the encampment and drove in. The blue tents were scattered all around the campsite and three large white trailers were grouped together on one side. Ramón drove on the perimeter of the tents to see if there were people around. A door from one of the trailers opened and two men stepped out. They were similarly dressed in long khaki shorts and hiking boots. One of the men had a rough gray beard and was looking into a notebook. The other man had a long ponytail tied at the back of his neck and was checking his glasses for smudges. Both men looked up from their activities at the same time and saw the scooter drive up.

"Hey, could you tell us where the next campsite is?" Ramón had stopped Natalie within a few feet of the men.

The men looked with curiosity at the two boys on the dusty old scooter. The bearded man spoke first.

"Where are you headed to?"

"We're headed to Santa Fe, but we need a place to stop for the night," replied Ramón.

The bearded man glanced off toward the interstate thinking about the great distance to Santa Fe, then refocused his attention on the two young faces in front of him.

"Are you traveling alone?" he asked.

"Yeah, my brother and I are meeting our parents in Albuquerque tomorrow." Ramón lied quickly, afraid of what Miguel might say.

The bearded man turned his head slightly in bewilderment at the boys' situation. His thoughts had been occupied by the importance of the project he was working on and suddenly his mind had been forced to turn to the predicament of two children. He looked to the man standing next to him for his opinion on the subject.

The younger man with the ponytail smiled and asked the boys if they had been eating and if they had found a place to sleep the night before. The boys responded that they were taking care of themselves on the road. The younger man recognized the adventurous spirit of the boys and nodded back to the older man, suggesting his consent to have Miguel and Ramón join the group.

"I don't mind if they stay. I'll take the responsibility, Dr. García," the younger man said generously.

"If you have your own gear you can stay here for the night. We have a tent that's not in use and I'm sure the other boys won't mind." He took a few steps forward and introduced himself. "I'm Dr. García and this is Dr. Shaw. We're heading up this dig. The others will be back soon."

Ramón held out his hand to shake Dr. García's hand and introduce himself. Miguel dismounted the scooter and copied the actions of his cousin.

"We won't get in the way. We can set up our stuff anywhere," Ramón said, suddenly feeling shy.

"Why don't you and Miguel drive over to the last tent by the second fire pit, I'll have one of the boys help you as soon as they return," said Dr. García. He kept a stern expression on his face while he spoke but Ramón could see that he was a generous man. Dr. Shaw smiled at the boys through his cloudy lenses. He was closer in age to the boys than Dr. García and recognized their need for adventure.

Ramón and Miguel drove Natalie to where they had been told and untied their backpack and sleeping bag. Miguel was glad to have a safe place to sleep that night and Ramón was intrigued about the idea of a dig.

"What are they digging for?" Ramón thought to himself as they walked around the vacant blue tent. "Could there be buried treasure in the desert?"

Miguel went to look for wood to start a fire as Ramón's fascination with the desert and all its hidden mysteries grew.

chapter 30

"Are we supposed to be burning stuff in there?" Ramón asked Miguel.

Miguel had started a large fire in the fire pit and was standing back from the high flames, admiring his achievement.

"It's going to be dark soon and cold. Last night was real cold," Miguel said, remembering how he had shivered all night without a sleeping bag to sleep in.

"What are you guys doing in here?" a voice suddenly said from outside the tent.

Ramón stood up and turned to see a young man dressed in dirty jeans and a straw cowboy hat.

"Who are you?" Ramón boldly asked in return.

"I'm Scott, and you're in my tent," the tall blonde man said, removing his hat and looking around at the boy's belongings. "Who put you in here?"

"We'll put up another tent, Scott. They need a place to sleep tonight. Why don't you get Randy over here to help set it up?" Dr. Shaw shifted his dirty glasses over his face to the top of his forehead.

The young scientist was average in height and lanky. Ramón liked him.

"I'm sorry, man, we'll move our stuff," Miguel said, standing up next to Scott, inadvertently showing everyone in the tent that he was just as tall as the young blonde man.

Scott took a step back from Miguel and nodded his head to Dr. Shaw's request. He wasn't expecting Miguel to act so maturely.

Dr. Shaw motioned for the boys to leave the tent and bring their stuff outside with them. He stood next to the burning fire pit to warm his thin body and said, "We'll get you set up right now. Randy is a pro at setting up these tents."

"Thanks, Dr. Shaw, we really appreciate this," said Ramón, hoping Randy would arrive soon. He suddenly felt tired from the drive and his left arm had started to hurt again.

"You can call me Greg. 'Dr. Shaw' sounds like my dad," he laughed.

"Greg, do you guys eat dinner. I mean, could we buy dinner if you have some extra?" Miguel was feeling his stomach start to growl with hunger.

"We have plenty, don't you worry. We all get hungry out here working like we do. We won't leave you out," he promised. Then, seeing another young man approach, he added, "Ah, here's Randy. He'll get you set up. See you later."

Randy was short for an adult and thickly built. He had stocky, muscular legs and his long khaki shorts were almost the length of regular pants on his short frame. He quickly unfolded a thick square of blue canvas and spread it out over a new piece of flat ground.

"Can we help?" Miguel said, picking up the metal poles he saw lying on the ground. "I've set up a tent before. Where do you want these?"

Randy tipped the brim of his baseball cap up on his forehead and looked at Miguel. "Yeah, put those over by the corners of the tent and bring me the sledgehammer by my pack."

His strong, wide hands took a firm grip around the hammer and he pounded in the metal stakes, then fitted the poles in place. He didn't speak again to the boys until the tent was finished. Randy stood back, put his rugged hands on his thick waist, and commented, "That's how you pitch a tent." He then picked up his pack and hammer and walked off toward the other end of the camp.

"When do you think we're gonna eat?" asked Miguel, moving the backpacks and sleeping bag into the newly constructed tent.

Ramón sat on the ground and moved the sleeping bag over to rest his head. "My arm is really sore. It's probably good that we stopped. I don't think we would have made it all the way to Albuquerque by tonight."

"Yeah, but these guys don't seem too friendly. That Scott guy looked like he wanted to take a swing at me," Miguel said, remembering that there was an uneaten granola bar in his backpack. "I mean, what if they decide they don't want us here and we have to leave in the middle of the night?"

He ripped open the paper wrapper and bit into the oatmeal-and-raisin bar with a concerned look on his face. He couldn't help thinking about the possibility of another cold night in the desert.

"We'll be all right. We're in their territory, remember. No one invited us," Ramón answered.

Miguel chewed on the granola bar and kept wondering what they would eat for dinner that night.

"I wonder what Tío is having at his barbeque. Do you think they'll have steaks?"

Ramón laughed as he nodded off to sleep. Safe in the blue tent, he dreamed that he was digging for buried treasure in a far off land and that Miguel was eating the biggest steak that he had ever seen.

chapter 31

Miguel opened his eyes to see a small spot of light shining through the translucent blue fabric of the tent. He hadn't meant to fall asleep, but after Ramón had gone unconscious, he had laid down to rest his tired legs and, before he knew what was happening, he was asleep too. He glanced around the dark interior of the tent in search of his backpack, and upon seeing it in the corner, he slid it over and took out the flashlight.

Shining the bright light directly into Ramón's face he said, "Hey, man, get up, we're going to miss dinner!"

Ramón slowly opened his eyes despite the brightness of the flashlight's bulb.

"What are you doing? Go back to sleep," he said, turning his body over to the other side.

"It's not time to sleep yet, Ramón. Get up. I mean it. I'm hungry," Miguel said, standing up and opening up the flap to the tent. In the distance he could see the young men starting to take their seats around a campfire and eating from their plates. "Come on, get up," he pleaded with his cousin.

Ramón sat up and looked out the opening of the tent. He considered not eating dinner, but then remembered that they didn't have any more food in their backpacks. "All right, let's go," he said.

They walked over to the group and Dr. Shaw noticed them first. "Hey, there, come on over and have some dinner."

Dr. Shaw motioned for the two boys to join the group. "Scott made spaghetti tonight with his special sauce."

Tipping his cowboy hat away from his forehead to get a better look at Miguel and Ramón, Scott said, "Hope you like snake meat." A few of the other guys laughed and kept eating from their plates.

Miguel looked into the large pot of spaghetti with a worried frown.

"Don't worry, Scott's kidding with you," Greg interjected. "Grab a plate."

Miguel decided to believe that the spaghetti was safe to eat and piled his plate with the long noodles covered in meat sauce. The two boys sat on two empty folding chairs facing the center fire and started to eat.

"So what did Dr. García say when you told him what we found?" asked Scott, directing his question to Greg.

"He's concerned that we don't disturb an ancestral burial site. He's going with us tomorrow to check it out for himself," Greg replied.

"According to my research, the canyon we were in today could very well contain the foundations of the ancient city we have been looking for," spoke another young man named Adam.

Adam was the group's smartest member and had been nicknamed "The Brain" back in high school. Adam knew everything about everything and his knowledge was invaluable to the expedition.

"Hey, Brain, did you see the cave leading from the watering hole, the one that was blocked by the large rock? I think we should check that out first thing tomorrow. Maybe the rock was put there to keep intruders out. It could be hiding something important," Scott said, excited about the next day's adventure.

Brain opened his laptop and typed in some information. He always kept his computer with him. He researched everything that he discovered and was always eager to share his new information with his teammates.

"According to the last geological survey . . . "

Brain continued to explain his scientific theory regarding the second cave until Scott interrupted him. "Hey, I bet that computer didn't tell you we would find a body down there, did it?"

Ramón had been following their conversation and was caught by surprise at the mention of finding a dead body in a canyon. He looked at the tall cowboy and hoped he would continue with more details about the morbid discovery.

Brain didn't respond. He was busy typing into his computer. His fingers moved at a rapid pace and his concentration was intensely focused on his project.

Dr. Shaw had finished eating and was looking in the direction of the three white trailers. He thought of the conversation he'd had just a few minutes before they started to eat dinner. Dr. García was not pleased that a body had been found at the dig site. The archaeological expedition was planned for research only and not for excavation. The team had just arrived two days earlier and now that an important discovery had been made, Dr. García would have to acquire new permission from the Native American people that they had been working with. It was their land and one of their ancestor's physical remains had been unearthed. Dr. Shaw looked into the campfire and thought of the responsibility that they all shared to respect the history of the land and the importance of scientific research.

"Greg," Scott shouted, "what do you think of the mummy we found?"

Ramón felt a shiver go down his spine. The thought of a mummy was even more exciting than a dead body.

"We just don't know what else is down there, Scott. Tomorrow we'll learn more," Greg said, still concerned with Dr. García's reaction.

Ramón had been quiet but eventually blurted out, "So is the mummy all wrapped up like they do in Egypt?"

Greg looked up from his thoughts and answered Ramón's question.

"Every civilization has a different method of burying their dead. We can learn a lot about a culture's beliefs and customs by examining the remains." He stopped for a moment then added, "Why don't you and Miguel come along tomorrow?"

Ramón's heart raced at the thought of participating in a real expedition that searched for mummies and old relics. He quickly replied, "Yeah, that would be cool!"

After his hasty response, Ramón considered that he and Miguel needed to continue their drive to Santa Fe. He looked at Miguel and thought of the opportunity for adventure, an opportunity that might never come again. Taking the last bite of spaghetti on his plate, he decided they would stay. The thought of hidden treasures in the desert was too great a temptation to resist.

chapter 32

The morning came quickly and before Miguel or Ramón could fully open their eyes Randy was at their tent telling them that they had five minutes to pack up for the hike into the canyon gorge. Miguel adjusted his T-shirt and put on his jacket. The morning air felt cool and there was a slight breeze blowing against the flimsy tent walls. Ramón was slower to wake up. He had slept deeply and didn't remember where he was. They both laughed at Ramón's confusion and picked up their backpacks to join the expedition team. All the guys were standing around the morning campfire drinking coffee and eating bread rolls with sandwich meat.

"You boys drink coffee?" asked Greg, holding out a cup of steaming dark liquid to Miguel.

"Okay," Miguel said, accepting the coffee. He wasn't used to the taste of coffee but it felt good to drink something hot.

Greg gave the boys two of the sandwiches and told them of the precautions they would need to take that day. "It's important you stick with one of us at all times for the entire day. We can't watch out for you and get our work done at the same time, so stay close. Remember, safety first."

Miguel and Ramón nodded their heads in acknowledgment of the rules and finished their coffee and sandwiches quickly.

The sun was just appearing over the distant mountains and the desert glowed with new life. Small colorful flowers opened as the sunlight began to spread upon the open plain and the creatures that had roamed freely during the blackness of the night buried themselves in safe places. The emptiness of the desert was an illusion. Life existed in all forms and in the aged depths of time ancient civilizations breathed. The desert was a place full of history and remembrance.

Miguel zipped up his jacket and adjusted his backpack. It felt lighter since they had consumed all of their food and water. Greg gave the two boys several bottles of water for the day and reassured them that they would eat lunch. Miguel thought about the snake meat in the spaghetti and wondered if Scott cooked all the meals.

Ramón followed behind Miguel as the long hike commenced. They would have to walk half a mile to the entrance of the canyon, then make the deep descent into the gorge. The team's dig site where the mummy had been found was a considerable distance from the canyon entrance. Ramón walked quickly in line with the team of explorers and listened to their conversations with rapt attention.

"On a hunt through Yellowstone, my brother and I ran into the biggest grizzly you have ever seen. You know that bear that they use in all those movies? Well, our grizzly was twice as big, and boy when he saw us, I thought we were done for." Scott had begun his story after being asked about bears in his home state of Wyoming.

"He came running after us with amazing speed. You can't imagine how fast they are! He was like a massive truck barreling downhill at us!" Scott exclaimed.

Ramón thought of the big-rig trucks on the interstate and imagined the gigantic bear roaring down the highway chasing them on the scooter.

"Thank God Kevin was a good shot. The bear tumbled over himself and landed just five feet in front of us!" he added.

"The velocity of a moving object at full speed, once adjusted for the weight . . . " Brain was busy calculating the weight of the grizzly based on the distance of the brothers and the incline of the hill. He did the calculation in his head and soon arrived at an impossibly correct estimation. "That bear was approximately twelve hundred pounds!" he proudly announced.

"At least that, maybe more," Scott bragged.

Miguel looked at Scott and asked candidly, "Weren't you scared? I mean, did you think you were gonna die?"

"We all gotta go sometime," Scott quipped bravely. Then, in an instant, his expression changed from braggart to quiet grief. He lowered the brim of his cowboy hat over his eyes and walked looking down at the desert floor, adding only a few more words, "You never know what's going to happen. If I had known . . . "

Miguel noticed the change in the cowboy's voice and didn't ask more questions. He turned to Greg who had been on the phone with Dr. García, "How many digs have you been on?"

Dr. Shaw folded up the cell phone and attached it to the clip on his khaki pants. Dr. García was joining the team after lunch. He was meeting with the tribal chief to inform him of the previous day's discovery and to ask for permission to continue with the excavation. Dr. Shaw hoped that the team could continue with their research. He was eager to make a name for himself and to be respected in the field like Dr. García was. He turned to Miguel and replied, "This is my fourth dig in the southwest desert, but I've also been on expeditions to Mexico and South America."

Miguel was impressed. Dr. Shaw was a real explorer, traveling the world looking for important discoveries. "So how long did you go to college to become a doctor?" he asked.

"Well, first I finished my undergraduate work, then I enrolled for my graduate studies. In total about eight years," Dr. Shaw said casually.

"Wow, that long? Did you always want to be an archae-ologist?" Miguel added.

"Well, actually I consider myself a scientist, sometimes an anthropologist. I study people, how they lived, their customs," he answered, reflecting on his own self image. "I was always interested in history and people in ancient civilizations. When I saw pictures of ancient Egypt and the ancient Meso-American cultures, I could imagine myself back in time, living like they did."

Miguel had never seriously considered the daily customs and rituals of ancient cultures before. He had been a good student at school and his history classes had interested him the most, but the last few years had been different. School wasn't exciting anymore. He didn't enjoy reading the out-dated textbooks and listening to hours of memorized lectures. His grades were below average, and it worried him. He knew that he couldn't play soccer if he didn't maintain good grades.

"Why couldn't school be exciting like this?" he thought to himself. He then decided he would tell his next history teacher that the class should take a field trip through the desert to see what he saw, history before his eyes.

The team of explorers and scientists continued their walk through the desert terrain toward the canyon.

chapter 33

The rim of the canyon was not visible until the team had crossed over the last small ridge that ran through the desert floor. Greg led the team down the narrow descent into the canyon gorge, slowly pacing the others and bracing himself against the strong rock formations which had formed walls on each side of the climb. Miguel and Ramón kept their eyes on the stone steps and always had at least one hand on a stone wall. As the rocky staircase widened toward the bottom of the gorge, the walls opened up and a valley full of green foliage was displayed. Short leafy trees grew in groups and a steady stream of mountain water ran through the valley floor. The team continued their hike past the verdant valley and began a short climb that led into a rock wall.

Greg noticed a figure waving from the top of a cliff they were approaching and commented, "That must be Eric. I see he survived the night up here."

"He's never been the same since the Nepal expedition," observed Scott, adjusting his daypack and fastening a hunting knife to his thick leather belt. "He's always meditating. What happened up on that trip, anyway?" he questioned Brain, who was walking last in the group.

Brain didn't respond. He was too busy calculating the changes in desert temperatures for the last three centuries.

Eric walked easily from his superior position on the cliff and quickly joined the others. He was dressed in jeans and a long-sleeved white T-shirt. He slung a daypack from one shoulder and a strange drum-like instrument from the other. His hair was raven black and hung loose over his shoulders.

As he walked toward the team of young men, his tanned face held an expression of quiet contentment and peace.

"How did it go up there?" asked Greg, stopping and looking at Eric.

"The canyon spoke to me last night," he replied with a distant look on his face.

"Did it tell you where we should dig?" quipped Scott, laughing as he passed Greg on the path.

Eric ignored the cowboy's remarks and took a large breath of air. He glanced at Miguel and Ramón for a moment then proceeded to follow the group. The others followed and soon arrived at their destination. Carved into the cliff wall was a mass of stone and clay buildings. They were square in shape and had flat roofs with large doorways cut into the walls. Miguel and Ramón looked at the structures with curiosity and followed Greg to one side of the established dig site.

Dr. Shaw was hesitant to begin excavating again without Dr. García's approval. He split the group into three teams and took Miguel and Ramón with himself, Scott, and Eric to the edge of the cliff wall, and instructed Scott to continue to clear the area slowly. Scott took his hunting knife from his belt and set it beside his work space. Eric unrolled a leather bundle containing various sized brushes and small sharp blades. Miguel and Ramón sat off to the side of the two archaeologists and watched each movement they made with interest.

"So, what are you guys looking for? If there are more dead bodies would they be right here?" Miguel asked, moving closer to Scott to see what he was doing.

"No, kid, no bodies here. We'll have to wait til Dr. García gives us the go-ahead to continue that part of the dig. Now we're looking for small artifacts."

"Are you a doctor, too?" continued Miguel.

"Almost. This research project should do it, then everyone can call me Dr. Harris." He looked up from his work and smiled to himself. "I'm going to like that. 'Dr. Harris.' Sounds important."

Miguel watched the slow, gradual process that Scott and Eric were involved in. Their dig site was only a few feet wide and they cautiously checked each clump of dirt with their knives and brushes, hoping to find a hidden treasure. They filled the slow early morning hours by talking about their past adventures.

"Remember the pottery we found last year?" asked Eric moving his long hair back away from his face. "If we had our doctorates then, we could have taken full credit for that find."

"Yeah, I heard they're going to be part of an international exhibition in New York," answered Scott, picking up his knife to carve a deeper hole on his side of the site.

Eric stopped brushing the large clump in his hand and said to Ramón, "What brought you two here?"

"It was Miguel's idea, we needed to stop for the night," he answered looking with interest.

Eric looked into the blue morning sky, then back to Ramón.

"Something must have brought you here. There are no accidents in this world." He grinned and began to brush the object in his hand delicately.

Ramón thought about Eric's words.

Dr. Shaw walked over to their group. He took a long drink from his water bottle and told Scott, "Dr. García will be here in a few hours. Let's hold off on this site until we know if we can continue with the one in the cave."

Scott and Eric nodded and put away their tools. The boys stood up and walked over to the other group working nearby to observe their activities. Randy was using a large shovel to start a new dig site and Brain was opening his laptop. After looking up for a moment at the boys, Brain continued with his work. He connected a battery power pack to the side of the computer and began typing.

"Can we watch for a while?" Miguel asked.

Randy looked up at Miguel and told him to start moving the loose dirt onto the metal sieves. "Just move the bowls around back and forth. If you see something that's not just dirt, tell us," he ordered, more concerned with the digging of the hole than the scientific aspects of the project.

"Look, Ramón," Miguel said, shaking the round metal bowl back and forth, "it's like panning for gold. Remember that camping trip with Grandpa when I found a gold nugget?"

Ramón picked up another metal container and joined his cousin in the search for the precious gold.

From outside of the cave opening, Miguel saw Dr. Shaw waving at the two boys to stop what they were doing and come over to where he was. The boys put down their sifting bowls and went outside.

"Since Dr. García won't be here for a while, Eric has agreed to take you through another cave site. Do you want to go?" asked Dr. Shaw.

"Yeah," Ramón answered quickly.

"I'm sending Randy and Scott along too," Dr. Shaw added, looking at Eric. "You're in charge. Be careful out there."

The newly assembled team of five walked out of the gorge site using the same path that they had taken earlier that morning. They continued back to the stream and cluster of trees and crossed over the shallow water to the other side of the canyon. There Scott pointed to the cave that had caught his curiosity the day before.

"That's it," Scott said, pointing to a small, dark opening that was blocked by a large boulder. "That's our cave!"

"We have to move that boulder before we can get in. Any ideas, guys?" Eric asked, including Miguel and Ramón in the question.

"We need leverage, something to tilt it from the bottom, then we can push it over to the side," said Scott.

They all agreed that Scott's idea might work. They looked around for a strong piece of wood to use, something that wouldn't break under the pressure of the large boulder. Ramón found it first.

"Hey, would this work?" he asked, holding up a sturdy wood branch.

"Let's try it," said Scott, taking the branch and lodging it underneath the rock.

The branch was slid under the rock as far as possible, then Scott and Eric tried to push the rock away from the cave opening. The rock didn't budge.

"Randy, do you think you can try?" asked Scott.

Randy braced himself against the boulder and bent his knees. Miguel walked over and took the same position against the rock next to Randy. "Let's push on three," the boy said to Randy.

With the leverage of the branch and the strength of two men, the boulder was moved away from the opening. The cave was now open to exploration and the young men entered, not knowing what they would find.

chapter 34

The bright beams of the flashlights lit the dark walls of the cave as they walked deeper into the mysterious tunnel. Scott led the way. He took out his knife and held it in his right hand, ready to use it. The cave was narrow and after walking for a few minutes, a large underground room appeared. The team entered the cavernous room filled with shadows and stood in surprise at what they saw. The walls of the room were painted with large colorful pictures of people, animals, and hunting scenes.

"What have we found?" whispered Scott in complete shock.

"This must be one of the caves I've been reading about," Eric started to explain. "The theory is that these caves were used in rituals for the young boys of the tribe."

"What kinds of rituals?" asked Ramón, wondering if he was the right age.

"Rites of passage, actually," said Eric. "The men of the tribe would lead the young boys, probably about your age, down into these caves to initiate them into their society. It was meant to teach them of their responsibilities of being a tribal member and to scare them a little, too."

"Why would they want to scare them. Was it like punishment?" asked Miguel.

"Adulthood was a serious responsibility for these ancient tribal cultures. They had to be sure that the young boys would respect nature and put the needs of the tribe first, above their own," answered Eric.

"These wall paintings must be over one thousand years old," commented Randy. "How did they see to paint. There's no light in here."

Miguel and Ramón walked up to the painted walls and stared at the colorful and familiar forms. The figures of people were painted in geometric shapes and the animals were large and fierce looking. Many of the paintings were scenes of men hunting animals with arrows and spears. The cave felt magical, as if something very important had happened there a long time ago.

Scott walked around the room and saw another passage leading upward. "I'm going to check this out," he said, starting to climb out of the cave.

"We should all go together. We don't know where that passage leads," advised Eric. "You two follow Scott and Randy," he said, pointing to Miguel and Ramón.

The passage was dark but a small amount of light was filtering in and they didn't need to use their flashlights. Scott was a quick climber and Miguel followed close behind. Suddenly Miguel heard a noise that sounded like a rattle, then a hiss.

Scott, hearing the noise too, stopped climbing and told Miguel to step back. Then it appeared on a crevice of the wall, a rattlesnake, coiled in a corner posing to strike Miguel.

"Don't move," Scott said in a quiet voice. "He'll strike if you move suddenly. Stay back and keep your eyes on him."

Miguel was terrified but did what Scott told him. He took a slow breath and waited. Scott slowly raised his knife and aimed at the head of the snake. With one fast throw, the knife lodged in the snake's neck and it was dead.

Scott cut the snake's head off and cleaned the bloody blade on his pants. "Well, looks like more snake meat tonight, guys!" he laughed.

Miguel looked at the headless long body and knew the terror that must have existed in that cave years ago.

"Look at this!" Scott yelled back. "It looks like this passage leads to the top of another formation."

The team of five climbed out of the passageway one by one, out into the daylight. As they glanced around they saw that they were standing on top of the tallest cliff in the canyon. The view was spectacular. The desert floor expanded beyond the canyon walls into the horizon in all four directions. They were standing on top of the world. Miguel and Ramón stood on the cliff taking in the view, turning their bodies to see the desert that surrounded them.

"It looks like we're at the center of the earth, that everything revolves around us," Ramón observed.

Eric smiled and looked at Ramón thoughtfully. "There are many centers. I have stood on the tallest mountains all over the world and have felt just as you do now."

The five young men stood together on the top of the cliff, each feeling that he was a part of something greater than himself.

chapter 35

"Dr. García, what's the word?" shouted Scott as he saw Dr. García ascending the pathway. The five explorers had returned to the first cave full of stories about what they had seen that morning.

"Well," Dr. García started, a little out of breath from the climb, "looks like we can continue for now. The tribal council is making their final decision. They'll be joining us tomorrow at the site. They gave us permission to keep digging, but we can't remove anything today."

Dr. García removed his khaki brimmed hat and wiped the sweat from his forehead. As the leader of the expedition, he was responsible for the entire project. The meeting with the Native American tribal leaders had gone well but they needed time before they would consent to the removal of their ancestor's bones from the ground that they considered sacred.

"Last night the canyon told me it understood why we were here," interjected Eric, staring off into the distance.

Greg heard Eric's words, then said, "Okay, you heard it. Let's get moving to the cave." Then he turned to Dr. García. "We've located another cave with primitive wall paintings. It'll have to be investigated further."

Dr. García's eyes opened wide, "Another discovery in the same canyon?" He wiped his forehead again. "When the tribal leaders join us tomorrow, we'll check it out. This is miraculous. Good work, Dr. Shaw."

"It wasn't me. Scott, Eric, Randy, and . . . " Greg hesitated, "and our two boys were instrumental in getting access into the cave."

"Well, well. Looks like we have two archaeologists in training. Very good!" Dr. García laughed.

The team took their flashlights from their packs as they approached the entrance to the cave. From the top of the cave rays of sunlight filtered through a hole in the ceiling and the team stopped for a moment to regroup.

"Okay, let's begin where the body was found first, then we'll spread out and see what we find," Greg said, moving his flashlight around the room, directing the team.

Eric unloaded his pack and said a quiet prayer over the hole in the cave floor which until the day before had held the body of one of his ancestors. Scott took off his cowboy hat and lowered his head in silence until Eric had finished his reverent words.

Eric was sensitive to the desert. He was born into the Hopi tribe that lived nearby. Leaving his family to pursue his education had been difficult, and although it was hard to be far from his beloved land, he knew that his achievements in science had made the tribal elders very proud. He never forgot to thank his ancestors for his good fortune and for the wisdom that he had acquired in his life.

Dr. García paced around the room, glancing at the team of his students and at Dr. Shaw. Dr. García's accomplishments in science were impressive but his valued reputation among his peers was for the astonishing research and anthropological theories that he had produced in his thirty years of experience. He walked around the newly lit cave and reviewed the ground floor.

"What do you boys think of all this? I hear you've had quite an adventure this morning," Dr. García asked, looking at Miguel first then Ramón.

They were unaware of Dr. García's impressive credentials but knew by his voice and posture that he was an important man.

"This is really cool. I didn't think that this kind of stuff really happened. It's like being in a movie," Miguel gushed, looking at his cousin for something more to say.

"I like not knowing what you could find. It's kinda exciting, like anything could happen!" responded Ramón.

"Well, we research the history of the area before we start a dig, so we do know what it is we should be looking for. But sometimes we do find something surprising," answered Dr. García.

"Like the mummy?" blurted Miguel.

Dr. García smiled and thought of his own boyhood adventures. "Maybe you'll help us find another?"

Miguel and Ramón felt the rush of exploration run through their veins. Miguel recalled the books that he had at home about the history of the ancient civilizations and thought he would look through them again when he got back home.

Ramón was thinking of the people that must have lived in the canyon, in the stone buildings, and in the caves they were now exploring. "What if we could talk to one of them now? What would they say about us if they saw our cars, TVs, movies?" he thought to himself.

The boys leaned against the cave wall and watched the scientists at work. There was so much to discover about the world, lands to travel, and cultures to discover about. They realized that their lives had just begun, that the first fourteen years had been filled with the actions and thoughts of children, and that a new life with exciting possibilities was opening up to them. They were no longer just kids.

They continued to observe the men work in silence and thought about all the amazing things they would do when they grew up.

chapter 36

The day ended in triumph. Another ancient grave had been discovered in the cave and Dr. García shared that he thought they had made a significant scientific discovery. They all walked back to the campsite with their heads held high and boasting of who would win their first international award.

A huge fire was lit and dinner was soon ready. Dr. García had arranged for the delivery of a special dinner in celebration of their amazing discovery. Large aluminum trays were uncovered to reveal stacks of barbequed spareribs and corn on the cob. Everyone cheered at the bountiful feast. Miguel ate more than anyone else, piling his plate three times before most of the others had finished their first plate.

"Hey, man, you got your barbeque!" Ramón said, in a teasing voice, proud that his cousin could eat more than the older guys.

Miguel nodded his head and wiped the spicy sauce from his chin. "This is really good," he managed to say before taking another big bite.

"Hey, Eric, tell us one of your stories," bolted Scott. He had noticed Miguel eating more than anyone else and loaded his plate higher in competition with the young boy.

Eric wiped his sauce-stained fingers on a towel and placed his pack over to his side. He reached into it and pulled out an object which he purposely kept out of view. He then got up from his chair and began to speak.

"Usually you guys hear me tell a story that originated with my people and sometimes I tell a story that I have heard from faraway lands, but tonight I have a story that happened last night."

The small group stopped talking among themselves and listened to Eric as soon as he began to speak. He was considered to be a great storyteller and his stories were always filled with fascinating detail and magical surprises. Miguel and Ramón turned their eyes to the raven-haired man and felt the awe of mystery begin to surround the campfire.

"I had finished my evening stretches and had sat upon the great rock of the red-stained cliff. My mind was at peace and I felt the moon as she ascended into the heavens."

Eric extended his arms and gazed into the night sky as he spoke. The others watched every move he made and loved the dramatic interpretation that he added to his story. Scott sat back on his chair and kicked his feet up on a log sticking out of the fire. He grinned in enjoyment as Eric continued.

"The ground breathed beneath me, the walls of the canyon sounded their call to the desert, and I was one with the universe."

Eric then held his arms out along his sides and continued. "It was then that the Great Spirit revealed himself to me."

The listeners were stunned. Miguel stopped eating and Ramón felt the hair on his neck rise.

"He flew over the mountains and through the canyon, his wings spanned the width of the canyon walls, and when he landed on the cliff, his eyes met with mine."

Eric lowered one arm and bent his body slightly over to one side, then spun in a circle around the campfire. "The Great Spirit then allowed himself to be heard. He spoke of brotherhood and of the love a father has for a son."

Eric stood in front of Ramón and looked directly in the young boy's eyes. "He dropped this in my hands and told me that I would know to whom it belonged."

He drew a long white eagle feather from the inside of his jacket and handed it to Ramón. "This is yours. The Great Spirit is watching over you. Go in peace, my brother."

Ramón sat motionless in his chair. He reached for the majestic eagle feather as it was placed into his hands by the storyteller. He needed no further explanation. His heart told him the truth of the story.

Ramón held the feather to his beating heart and felt his father's presence. He had never left him. The dreams had always been real.

chapter 37

Sparks flew from the fire toward the night sky. The glow of contentment was on every face sitting around the flames. It had been a blessed day. After the story, Eric went back to his seat and lifted the drum that he had carried down from the cliff that morning onto his lap. He started to slowly tap on the stretched skin, closing his eyes to feel the rhythm of the moment.

Greg leaned over to the two boys and said in a hushed tone, "Eric has traveled on the Amazon. That's where he got that drum."

Seeing that the boys were fascinated by the origins of the music, he continued. "He went there with Brain and two former students on a research trip. I wish I had been there." The young man sighed and started to nod his head as the beats of the drum grew more distinct.

Dr. Shaw looked out into the night sky and remembered other nights that had felt like this one. He remembered nights after a day of discovery when the team of men felt cohesive and that along with the amazing new discoveries it had felt that anything in life was possible.

Eric continued to beat the drum and he began a low chant in the Hopi language. He had been the spiritual center of all the expeditions. His spirituality was invaluable to the group just as the genius of Brain, the independent spirit of Scott, and the hard work of Randy. Each one was important to the success of the project.

The drumbeats became steady. The others sitting in their chairs began to stare into the fire, losing their thoughts in the pulse of the drum. Brain, who had been sitting without his computer for the first time that day, went to his tent and returned with a set of round, wooden containers that made a rattling noise when shook. He sat next to Eric and shook the round objects in syncopation with the drumbeats. The music continued. Eric stood up and began to slowly shuffle his feet. Brain soon followed and within minutes all the others had joined. Eric continued to sing the traditional Hopi chant while they shuffled in a slow, steady dance in a circle, one after the other. With each slow step, they celebrated the day and they thanked the earth for giving them life.

Miguel and Ramón joined in the dance and kept the steady pace with the others, feeling like they had joined a special club. They would never forget these nights in the desert where everything seemed possible.

chapter 38

The road continued to Santa Fe. Natalie's small engine hummed along the interstate highway with the two boys safely on board. Although Miguel and Ramón had been on their journey for several days, they still had a long way to go. Before they left the campsite, Dr. Shaw had refueled the Vespa and given them bottled water and snacks for the road.

"You boys be careful. You should get to Albuquerque in a few hours if you drive steady," Dr. Shaw advised.

"Thanks, Greg, I can hardly wait to tell everybody what we saw!" said Miguel.

"You boys just stay on track and maybe some day, we'll see you out here again," Greg said with a smile.

The young men waived goodbye and Natalie sped away toward the interstate.

Miguel had decided to drive that morning and Ramón was behind him, absorbing the passing landscape. The mid-morning sun was bright and warm, illuminating a desert that was alive and endless.

"How much further do you think we have to go?" asked Miguel, turning his head slightly to speak to his cousin.

"The last sign said a hundred miles, I think," Ramón answered.

They had passed a road sign on the side of the highway but Ramón couldn't remember how long ago it had been or how many miles they had driven since seeing the sign. Both boys had adjusted to the idea of driving on the endless highway for as long as it took to get to Santa Fe. They knew that they would get there eventually.

chapter 39

odrigo sat at the kitchen table staring out of the window. The road that led up to his sister's house was visible from where he was sitting and since early that morning he hadn't been able to move.

They had reached Santa Fe the day before. And as soon as they arrived at his sister's house, Rodrigo called his mother to check on the boys but no one had answered. After several frantic calls to the police and finally to the town's hospital, he discovered what had happened to his mother. Now the boys were missing.

"I can't eat anything right now!" he shouted, shoving the plate of food away from him. A large cup of coffee was in his hand and he drank from the cup anxiously.

"You haven't eaten anything since we got here. If you eat, maybe your headache will go away," pleaded Connie. She was worried, too. While her husband had been on the phone all night trying to locate the boys, she had been crying and praying, hoping that they would see them again.

"I should have never left them behind. They didn't even have a phone to call us!" he said, admonishing himself. "What was I thinking?"

"We didn't know Rosa would get sick. How could we know?" responded Connie, stirring the pot of *menudo* on the stove.

"At least I know my mom will be okay," sighed Rodrigo. He took a drink of the coffee and picked up his cell phone. "Yes, I need the person in charge of missing children. I spoke to an Officer Martínez a few hours ago and I want an update," Rodrigo said in a commanding voice.

"Sir, Mr. Martínez is on a call right now. We can transfer you to the officer who coordinates that department," the voice replied.

"I need answers! My boys are missing. They could be in trouble somewhere!" shouted Rodrigo.

"The officer on duty can help you. Let me transfer the call."

Rodrigo spoke to the officer who did not give him any news. Overnight the police had checked his mother's house and the surrounding area, looking for Miguel and Ramón. No one remembered seeing them. After the preliminary investigation, the police had suggested that Rodrigo wait in Santa Fe to hear from the boys, who eventually would call.

When Rodrigo heard this suggestion from the police, he went into a rage. He yelled into the phone and told them they were incompetent for not being able to locate two young boys in a small town. He had spent the rest of the night pacing around the house between phone calls to police stations to all the towns between his mother's house and Santa Fe.

Rodrigo's sister and her family had been sleeping in the back bedrooms. Everyone had been up during the night to check on the progress of the police and to comfort Rodrigo who was taking it the hardest. Connie suggested to her husband that he lower his voice so that he wouldn't awaken the rest of the family.

Suddenly the loud ringing of the phone pierced through the kitchen.

"Hello, hello?" Rodrigo answered anxiously.

"*Mijo*, it's me," said the soft voice.

"Mamá, are you okay?"

"*Sí, claro*, the doctors are just being cautious, they tell me I'll be home soon. Are you okay? Your voice sounds upset."

"*Ay*, Mamá, I shouldn't tell you this but . . . "

Connie rushed to her husband's side and motioned for him to not say anything further to upset his mother.

"She might know something, Connie, I have to . . . " he said.

"What happened, *mijo*? Are the boys okay?"

"Mamá, when you went into the hospital, do you remember anything? Did you see the boys?"

"What's happening?" Abuela Rosa insisted.

"Nobody knows where they are. They've been missing for days!" Rodrigo confessed.

"*Mijo*, calm down," reassured Abuela Rosa. "They are in God's hands."

"Mamá, I'm so worried, what if something bad happened?" he muttered.

"While I was asleep, I had a vision that Miguel and Ramón were on a long trip."

"You mean like they were dead?"

"No, *mijo*, on a journey to find themselves." Abuela Rosa's voice was calm and thoughtful. "Your father has been speaking to me in my dreams and he told me that he was watching over them."

"Mamá, I want to believe that everything is going to be okay, but anything can happen to young boys alone in the world!"

"I know, *mijo*. You must have faith that they will find their way. God will provide for their safety. Just hold on to that thought."

Rodrigo heard his mother's words but he hung up the phone not feeling the reassurance that was intended.

"Where could they be?" he mumbled, resting his aching head on his hands.

"God will look after them, no matter where they are. He will protect them," Connie replied.

"That's not helping," Rodrigo roared. "It's my fault that they're lost, it's all my fault!"

"*Mi amor*, how could you know what would happen?"

"You don't understand, Connie. You don't know every-thing."

A sudden pang shot through Connie's heart when she heard her husband's words. She wiped her hands on a towel and asked, "What did you do?"

"Enrique wasn't supposed to drive to the store the night he died. It's my fault!" Rodrigo confessed as he clutched the coffee cup and his eyes began to fill with tears. "My dad had asked me to go. He needed something to fix the truck or else he couldn't go to work the next day, but I refused, I told Enrique to go."

"The accident wasn't your fault. That other car was dri-ving on the wrong side of the road," Connie said, remembering the night of the terrible accident.

Both brothers had been visiting their parents over the weekend with their young families. Miguel and Ramón were both three years old. When the call came from the police informing them of the accident and of Enrique's death, everyone had felt the devastating news. Ramón had been in the car with his father but luckily had not been injured in the accident.

"You don't understand, Connie," he said again.

"What don't I understand?"

"My brother had been working two jobs." His voice cracked but he fought back the tears. "He hadn't slept for two days. I knew that he was too tired to drive." Rodrigo's voice broke and his emotions poured out the rest. "But I didn't care that he was tired, all I cared about was myself!"

Connie sat at the kitchen table and with one long sigh, let all the breath in her body escape. Her husband had never spoken of the night of the accident and the sudden confession shocked her.

"So you see, if Enrique hadn't been driving that night, he wouldn't have died, and Ramón would still have a father!" Rodrigo took a breath and added, "None of this would have ever happened!

"I swear, Connie, if I'm given a second chance with those boys, I'm going to do things differently. I've been wrong to be so hard. When I think of what my last words were to them . . . " His voice broke again and he took a deep breath to stop from crying. "I'll be a better father. I owe the boys that, I owe my brother that."

Rodrigo sat at the kitchen table in silence, looking out toward the road.

"*Mi amor*, I know in my heart everything will be fine. We should wait like the police told us. The boys will contact us if we wait long enough," Connie said, trying to comfort her husband.

"Wait for what? Wait for the police to call to tell me they're dead!" He shouted, recovering from his tears. "I'm going back to look for them. They have to be somewhere!"

Rodrigo stood from the table and paced around the kitchen nervously. "I'll leave right now and you will stay here with Marisol, just in case the police call."

Rodrigo packed quickly the things he would need for the trip back to his mother's house. As he was gathering the last of his belongings, he heard his daughter screaming.

"They're here! They're here!" Marisol's voice shrieked as she ran to the house.

Rodrigo ran to the kitchen window and saw a cloud of dust approaching from down the road. He ran outside to the front of the house and saw something he would have never imagined in his wildest dreams. Miguel and Ramón were driving up on his old blue vespa.

chapter 40

"Dad! Dad!" Miguel yelled from the road.

Rodrigo stood speechless as the Vespa drove up the driveway. The long-forgotten vision of his boyhood motor scooter had shocked him into silence. Marisol came running after her father and ran to the boys first.

"Miguel! Ramón!" she screamed with delight. "We thought you were dead!"

The boys laughed a confident laugh and patted their little sister on the head playfully.

"You're not that lucky, sis. Maybe next time," Miguel joked.

Connie had heard the commotion outside and walked quickly from the house, still holding a spoon in her hand. At the unexpected sight of the boys, she felt a rush of maternal affection flood her body and the tears began to flow. She hugged both boys and told them how much they were loved.

Miguel and Ramón hugged her back. Miguel spoke first, "Is Abuelita okay? Did you call the hospital?"

"Oh, yes, she's going to be fine!" Connie exclaimed. "We just spoke to her and she's doing just fine." Connie's tears overtook her voice and she stood away from the boys to weep into her apron.

The two young men looked at Rodrigo standing before them. Rodrigo's face contained the expressions of both relief and wonderment. Feelings of anger did not occur to him. He only felt joy at seeing his two boys alive. Trying to speak, he stopped himself. He knew that his words could not express what he felt in his heart at that moment. He took one step forward and lifted both arms toward Miguel and Ramón. The boys rushed into the long awaited paternal embrace and lingered in the acceptance and love that only a father can give.

chapter 41

All the neighbors could hear the joyous celebration taking place inside the house. The planned family reunion had been transformed to include the homecoming of two beloved sons. After calling Abuelita Rosa to tell her the good news, Rodrigo joined the large family who squeezed themselves into the kitchen to be with the boys.

Connie and her sister-in-law fussed over the boys, feeding them endless amounts of home-cooked food. Both Miguel and Ramón ate voraciously and between bites they told of their adventure.

"Tell 'em about the desert pools we found and about the cliffs we climbed," Miguel said proudly.

Shrieks of excitement sounded from the children and from an occasional adult when Ramón told of the adventures. Younger cousins huddled around their new heroes and begged for all the gruesome details of the desert mummy and the headless snake in the cave.

Rodrigo sat at the kitchen table and listened attentively at the recitation of the boys' adventures on the road. The marvelous tales of the Grand Canyon, the red rocks of Sedona, and the archaeological expedition impressed him. He could see and hear from their stories that they were no longer irresponsible boys but young men on their journey to manhood. And as his impressions of them changed, he realized that his behavior as a father needed to change as well.

Rodrigo had always taken the responsibility of raising the boys seriously and had wanted to be a good father, but he now knew that his ideas of strict discipline without understanding had led to the boys almost being lost.

Thinking of the tragic consequences that might have occurred, he felt grateful that he had been given a second chance to be a better father.

After the noisy and story-filled family dinner, Rodrigo asked Miguel and Ramón to join him outside to build a fire in the backyard. Rodrigo placed large logs in the outdoor furnace and watched patiently as the boys did the same. Rodrigo lit the furnace and stood back from the growing fire, thinking deeply about the last few days and all the emotions that he had felt.

"I want you both to know something." Rodrigo started slowly, not wanting to reveal the depth of emotion that was building up inside of him.

"You two young men are everything to me. When I thought something could have happened to you . . . " He stopped and cleared his throat, not wanting to let the tears fall.

"We were okay, Dad. Grandpa showed us how to camp in the desert and we had some money just in case things got rough," Miguel reassured.

Rodrigo put his right arm around Miguel then motioned for his nephew to be embraced by his left.

"I'm going to promise you that things will be different. I'm going to be a better father," he managed to say before his voice gave out.

"Maybe we can go on a trip sometime?" asked Miguel, unsure of his father's response.

Ramón quickly added, before his uncle could answer, "Yeah, the guys we met at the Grand Canyon invited us back next summer!"

Rodrigo smiled through his tear-filled eyes and promised that he would take them on another trip through the desert. He knew that he needed to be reminded of the adventure of manhood.

The flames began to burn high into the evening sky. The stars came into view and a pale moon was visible through a thin veil of clouds. Rodrigo looked up into the heavens and for the first time in his life felt the immensity of the universe and the challenges facing him as a father to two young men.

"There is so much to see and to learn," Rodrigo said to himself. "I'm just beginning."

High above in the branches of an old pine tree watched a noble eagle. His keen eyes saw everything below. He stretched out his strong, feathered wings, then took flight over the rough terrain, soaring through the canyons and into the imaginations of young men. With a graceful swoop, the Great Spirit landed atop the tallest rock, amid the beauty and magic of the desert.